D1710253

Lala

I slipped my shades over my hazel eyes to try and hide the sadness in them and the tears that threatened to fall from them. I didn't want Tre to see me cry. I didn't want him to know that after all of the shit that I'd talked and all of the rules that I had made up when we first started kicking it I had still managed to get caught up and fall for him. It was true though I had and I'd fallen hard. I guess that's why people are always saying that you shouldn't try to plan shit because it never works out the way that you plan. This right here was a prime example. We were only supposed to be sex buddies and nothing more. That was the point of the rules. No kissing! No cuddling! No quality time! Just sex! That way neither of us caught feelings. In the beginning we both played by the rules but as time passed the rules started to slowly but surely be forgotten. I tried my hardest to stick to them but we all know how that goes.

I glanced in my review through teary eyes at his lean frame

still standing in the same spot that I'd left him in watching me as I drove my 2010 black Maybach out of the hotel parking lot and out of his life forever. That's when it happened! I couldn't fight the tears any longer. They flowed freely down my cheeks and there was nothing that I could do to stop them. My heart was in a million pieces. I wanted to turn around, go back and tell him how I felt but I couldn't because the truth of the matter was that he had someone and he loved her very much. I knew the rules of the game that I had chosen to play before it started so now I had to deal with the consequences. I can't even front in this situation the consequences were a motherfucker! They always are when it comes to matters of the heart. Sometimes your heart can be your worst enemy because that motherfucker will deceive you every time! You can try all you want to fight what you know is there but it has a mind of its own.

I opened the console that was in between my seats and took out a tissue. I took my shades off and laid them in the passenger seat, dried my eyes and tried my best to concentrate on the road. I had a long trip ahead of me. I was headed to Danville, VA. I was leaving Boykins, VA and all of my feeling for Tre behind. I couldn't stay here as long as he was here it was impossible. What I felt for him was too strong for the two of us to continue to live in the same town. I needed some distance between him and I and a whole lot of it! I knew that if I stayed I wouldn't be strong enough to continue to fight what I was feeling. This man had me so open that I might show up on his doorstep and tell him that I love him and fuck his girl because I wanted him in my life and not just as a cuddy buddy but as my man. I'd say it and be prepared to deal with whatever came after that! I knew that I couldn't do that though. Tre would no doubt kill my ass if I tried some shit like that! I wasn't that type of chick though. I knew my position.

I turned up the radio and as my luck would have it One Love by Trey Songz was playing. Tre and I both loved us some Trey Songz. I turned the radio to another station. Fifteen minutes into my drive my cell started to ring. I didn't have to look at the screen to see who it was because Cuddy Buddy by Trey Songz ringtone was playing that told me it was Tre. I quickly debated on whether or not I should answer but it didn't take long for me to decide. I needed to hear his voice again one last time.

I pressed the send button and answered. "Hello."

"Hey bae-bae, you good?" He asked his deep baritone voice was filled with concern. "You didn't seem like yo'self when you left. You acted like something was bothering you."

"Yeah, I'm good." There was a brief silence as I hesitated for a moment and took a deep breath before telling him what I hadn't been able to say back at the hotel. "Tre…I-I'm on my way out of town and I won't be returning. I need to get away for a while to get my head straight."

"Say what? What are you talking about?" He asked. I assumed confused by what I'd just said. "Get away from what?"

"Boykins!" I paused and then continued. "You…us!"

"Me? Us? Why the fuck are you talking in riddles? " He snapped. He hated it when I would beat around the bush instead of just saying what was on my mind. "Lala, umma ask you one more time to tell me what the fuck you are talking about!"

Fuck it! What did I have to lose? I was leaving anyways. Why not just keep it one hundred with him like I always had. "I am leaving town as we speak. I put all of my stuff in storage and my clothes are in the trunk."

He cut me off. "What? You did what? What the hell did you do that for? You are starting to piss me off! For some reason I am starting to feel like I am missing something!" He paused but before I could say anything he asked. "Is this about some nigga?"

I was caught off guard by that question and for some reason I even felt a little offended. He knew for a fact that he was the only man that I'd been sleeping with for the past two years. "What? Hell no! I'm leaving because instead of sticking to the rules of the game I messed around and got caught up! I fell in love! And before you say anything I know that we weren't supposed to be like that but the shit just happened! It crept up on me! I mean one day we were just sex buddies and you were giving me some of the best sex that I've ever had and the next I was starting to feel shit for you that I wasn't supposed to!" I cried. The water works had started

5

again.

He was silent for a minute and then I heard him let out a sigh. "Damn Lala, I don't know what to say. I mean…" I could imagine him pulling on the hair under his chin which he always did when he was deep in thought or at a loss for words.

I swiped at the tears that were rolling down my cheeks. "You don't have to say anything Tre. It's all good. I just got caught up that's not your fault, it's mine. I wish you the best. Bye." I was too afraid to hear his response so I disconnected the call and turned off my phone. "Damn I am going to miss you!" I said out loud. I was already missing him and I hadn't even been driving thirty minutes yet.

In the year and a half that the two of us had been getting it in he had shown me some shit that niggas I'd dated five and ten years his senior had failed to show me. At the tender age of twenty-four his dick game was on point and had a bitch like me wide open and fienin' for another taste. He knew how to kiss my neck, nibble on my ears, caress my breasts, and stroke my clit in a way that would have my body on fire in just a matter of seconds! Sometimes all he had to do was look at me in a certain way and my panties would just melt off!

"Fuck!" I banged my fists on the steering wheel. I was so damn mad with myself for allowing myself to catch feelings for a nigga that wasn't mine!

I looked ahead of me and saw a sign saying that there was an Exxon coming up within the next two exits. I decided that I would stop there, fill up my tank and get some snacks for the road.

I turned into the parking lot of the Exxon and pulled up to the gas tank. I pulled down the sun visor so that I could look in the mirror. My face was a mess with a mixture of snot and tears. I took some more tissues out of my console and dried my eyes and cleaned my nose before getting out of the car. I went inside and got the things that I would need for my trip. After walking up and down the aisles gathering snacks and some drinks, I took all of my things up to the register.

The cashier was an older black lady. "Hey, young lady. How

are you today? Did you find everything okay?" She asked giving me a warm toothy smile.

"Yes ma'am I did and I'm fine. How about you?" I asked politely.

"Oh I'm fine baby. I'm just ready to get out of here so that I can get down to the Bingo Hall. I'm feeling kind of lucky tonight!" She laughed but I just smiled because I wasn't in a laughing mood. "Why are you looking so sad? You are way too pretty to be wearing such a sad expression."

A lump formed in my throat. I wanted to respond but I couldn't because just thinking about the reason for the expression that I was wearing made me want to breakdown right there in the store and cry my eyes out!

"Young lady, I don't know why you're upset but if it has anything to do with a man. Dry those tears and put a smile on that pretty face of yours because if he's meant for you then it will be but if not then you will just have to put it behind you and move on. I know that is easier said than done but it's the truth. Y'all young

8

people need to stop worrying yourselves with things that you can't change. One day when you are older like me you will realize that those things aren't even worth half the energy that you put into worrying about them." Just as she got those words out of her mouth a gentleman walked up to the counter to pay for his items. She added up my snacks and my gas and then took my credit card and swiped it. I signed the receipt and grabbed my bag.

"Remember what I said." She told me before I walked out of the store.

"I will." I replied.

When I stepped outside I looked up at the sky. Thick grey clouds covered the sky telling me that I would more than likely run into some rain. The weather seemed to match my mood. I put my bag in the car and then pumped my gas. The cashier's words kept echoing over and over in my head because I knew that what she'd told me was right. The only thing was she didn't know that the man I was sad over wasn't even mines. I was upset and heartbroken over someone else's man. A part of me wished that I had just continued to fight off Tre's advances and never gave in to them but the other part of me had no regrets at all.

I got in my car and headed down Highway 58 on my way to a fresh start. I drove two hours straight before pulling off the road and into a McDonalds. I grabbed my cell and my purse and went inside. After receiving my order I found a table near the window and turned on my cell. I dialed my mom's number. I knew that she was probably worried sick about me by now since she hadn't heard from me all day.

"Hey baby. I am so glad that you finally called me. I have been worried sick about you. I've tried to call you at least ten times but kept right on getting your voicemail." She rattled off as soon as she answered the phone.

I'd told her that I was leaving town and even shared with her the reason why. I didn't keep any secrets from my parents. I didn't feel the need to. They've always let me know that I could talk to them about anything whether it was good or bad. They were going to love me regardless. When I'd told them about Tre and I neither of them said anything at first. After they had digested it my mom told me that I was a grown woman and to do whatever I felt like I needed to do.

My dad on the other hand simply said. "You know that I love you baby girl but the truth is you were wrong to go out here and lay with somebody else's man. Ain't there enough mens out here that you don't have to be sharing one?" He'd taken his hat off and scratched his head. "You know karma is a female dog. What you do to someone always comes back to bite you! We raised you better than that! I know we did! Here you are in love with another woman's man and running away from your home and your job! That is just nonsense!"

I wasn't upset to hear my dad say those words because I knew that he was telling the truth. It did hurt though. I did feel a little bit bad for sleeping with him knowing that he had someone and I also knew that if I was her it would hurt me to find out that my man was having an ongoing affair with some other woman for two years but shit happens. I feel bad but I don't regret one minute of the time that Tre and I spent together. It wasn't all sex. We shared a lot more. We had a lot in common. We both enjoyed the same type of movies, TV shows, and foods. We could sit and talk for hours about different things. He was also my friend.

"Ma, I apologize for causing you to worry. I just called to let you know that I am fine and that I have about another hour of driving ahead of me before I get to Danville."

Once I reached Danville I was going to be staying with my cousin Nita. The two of us have always been really close. So when I told her about my situation she didn't hesitate to let me know that I could come and stay with her until I found a job and a place of my own. She understood why I wanted to get away and agreed that it was probably for the best. She was afraid that if I continued to live in Boykins and continued my relationship with Tre that eventually his baby mama was going to find out and there would be a big mess! Honestly I believed that his baby mama knew that Tre wasn't being faithful. We women always have a feeling that something ain't right when our man is creeping. Aside from that, there have been plenty of nights where he has called home and told her that he would be a little more late than usual because somebody didn't show up to work and he had to cover for them. That was his excuse at least twice a week so that he could be with me. No woman is that damn stupid! She had to know that something wasn't right!

"I'm glad that you are okay but I still wish that you had thought this through some more before you made a final decision. I know that you are grown and I know that I told you to do whatever you felt like you needed to do but baby running away from a problem doesn't solve it."

I really didn't feel like going into all of that. I'd made my decision to leave and whether or not it was the best decision it was still my decision.

"I understand everything that you are saying ma and I appreciate your advice but I really don't want to continue to talk about it." I looked down at my food and suddenly didn't have much of an appetite anymore. "Ma, I'm about to get back on the road again. I will call you back in a few."

I heard her let out a sigh. "Okay. I love you."

"I love you too." I pressed the end button and took a couple more bites of my sandwich before picking up my tray and dumping my food in the trash. I went to the bathroom to empty my bladder before leaving.

Once I was back inside my car I turned up the music and continued on my way.

Tre

Saturday morning rolled around and found me sitting on the sofa watching Saturday morning cartoons with my seven year old twin boys, TreShaun and TreQuan. That's right I started young. I was sixteen when Kisha came to me and told me she was pregnant, she was eighteen at the time. I can't lie I was scared to death of becoming a father. I didn't know shit about no babies but I did know that I was going to be there for my seeds.

My father raised me to be a man and to never walk away from my responsibilities. Even if I was a child myself I knew that now was the time to stand up and act like a man. Luckily for me, my uncle owned a barbershop so he gave me a job sweeping up hair and running errands for him. As time passed he taught me everything he knew and allowed me to cut all of the kid's hair that came in. That allowed me to stay in school and also work and help take care of my kids. My mom almost had a nervous breakdown when I told her that I'd gotten someone pregnant and with twins at that but she accepted it. It wasn't like she had much of a choice because the babies were coming regardless. Between my mother and Kisha's mother we had been blessed to never have to worry about a babysitter.

I sat there on the sofa with my sons watching TV but I wasn't paying attention at all to the show. I had too much other shit on my mind. I couldn't stop thinking about Lala and how she'd just packed up and left. When I'd called and she'd told me that she was on her way out of town I thought she was joking but when I heard her crying and then she told me the reason why she was leaving. I knew that it wasn't a joke.

I'd seen her feelings for me starting to change but I didn't think that it was so serious. I knew that something was wrong with her the night before at the hotel when we were together because she was extremely quiet and when I'd sexed her that night, for what I didn't know was the last time, she'd held onto me so tight as if she didn't want to ever let me go. Normally she would complain if I kissed her or tried to hold her.

She would always say, "Move boy we don't need to be doing all of that mushy lovey-dovey stuff, that's how people catch feelings! Now move!" But that night to my surprise after we'd finished getting it in she'd laid in my arms with her head on my chest. I didn't bother to say anything because I was enjoying the way that she felt in my arms but I was wondering to myself what had brought on the sudden change of her all of a sudden wanting to cuddle. Like I said before, that wasn't like her at all.

I shook my head trying to possibly shake away my thoughts. This shit was beginning to give me a headache. I don't even know why I was allowing it to fuck with me this much. She wasn't my woman. She was just my side chic.

I turned my attention back to the TV but that didn't help at all because Saturday morning cartoons was me and Lala's shit. At the age of twenty-eight and twenty-four, we were still two big kids at heart. I would go over to her house sometimes on Saturday morning and crawl into bed with her. We would lay back and watch all of the old cartoons that we both loved so much. Tom and

Jerry, The Flintstones, The Jetsons, and The Pink Panther.

Normally we'd end up tuning out the TV when it would get a little hot up under the covers. The two of us couldn't keep our hands off of each other whenever were together. Our sexual chemistry was off the meter! Her caramel 5ft.2in. frame was my personal playground. I loved everything about her body, from her sexy ass hazel eyes to those full lips of hers, her 36D's, wide hips and phat ass. She wasn't no skinny chic but she was nice and thick. She wasn't fat. She was packing a few extra pounds but wore it well. I didn't care if her stomach wasn't flat as a board, she was always a little self-conscious about her stomach, which to me wasn't even that big but to her it was. I would tell her all the time that it just gave me a little something extra to hold on to.

I am one of those men who just love women period. All shapes, sizes and colors. I love them. I appreciate all women and everything about them. That's why my ass is always getting caught up in some shit! My babymama, Kisha, has caught me cheating too many times to even count but for some reason she loves my ass so much that she always takes me back. Don't get it twisted I love her too, more than anything else in this world besides my parents and my kids. There is no other bitch out here that could take her place not even Lala. She's wifey, always has been and always will be. I just can't control my dick. I have been doing a lot better though because after I met Lala and we started kicking it, she and Kisha have been the only two women that I mess with. I let all those other chicks go. I feel like that's progress!

Kisha doesn't know anything about Lala. That is because Lala always played her position, never blowing up a nigga's phone nor doing some dumb shit like coming by my house. We are even friends on Facebook, she has never did any shit like write some fly shit on my wall or send my girl a friend request or inbox her some bullshit. She isn't like that and that is what I love about her. Besides, I've already warned her and let her know that if she ever does some shit like that I will fuck her up! I do what I do in the streets and whether it's wrong or right I let any bitch that I fuck with know not to bring any dumb shit my girl's way!

I got up and grabbed my pack of Newports and lit one up and then walked over to the window and looked outside. It was raining. This shit with Lala was driving me crazy! The more I tried not to think about her, the more she stayed on my mind. I'd tried to call her, text her, Facebook message her but she hadn't responded to anything. I didn't like the way she was carrying this shit at all! I felt like she could at least call or text and let me know that she was okay. I'd grown to care about her a lot over the past two years and so knowing whether or not she was okay was important to me.

I heard footstep coming down the hallway, I already knew that it was Kisha. She came into the room wearing a pair of red shorts, a black t-shirt and a pair of black socks. She walked over and kissed both boys on the head and then came over to me. She wrapped her arms around my slim waist and stood up on her tip toes to kiss me. I took the cigarette from my lips and kissed her.

"Good morning baby." She smiled up at me. Her red hair was pulled back into a ponytail. I loved her hair this color it was so sexy against her light complexion. Kisha was so light that she was damn near white. She was 5'4 and very petite. She has some of the prettiest hazel brown eyes that I'd ever seen. I am a man who love hazel eyes. They do something for me.

"Good morning sexy." I replied.

"Have y'all eaten yet?" She asked kissing me again and then gently caressing the side of my face.

"Yeah mama we ate cereals." Quan answered.

"Oh okay."

"If you keep on kissing me like that I'm gonna take you down the hallway to our bedroom and eat again." I whispered in Kisha's ear, while licking it with my tongue.

"Mmmm, boy you'd better stop." She whispered back. "The boys are awake."

"So...they aren't thinking about anything but those cartoons. Come on." I said tugging on her hand.

We slipped out of the living room and down the hall to our bedroom. I locked the door, undressed her and then laid her back on the bed. She eased her legs open, eyeing me with a wide smile on her lips. I crawled between her legs and dove right in head first. First, I licked the outside of her lips and then spread her pussy open with my fingers and licked up and down the inside of her lips. I licked and sucked on her clit as she moaned and squirmed.

"Damn Tre…that feels so good." She said with one hand one my head holding it in place to make sure that I didn't move as she gyrated her hips. "Mmmm…baby just like that."

I left her clit alone and inserted my tongue inside of her opening fucking her with it. Her juices were spilling out onto my tongue and I could tell that she loved what I was doing. I replaced my tongue with three fingers and her pussy gripped them tightly as I moved them in and out of her nice and slow. I zone back in on her clit and started licking and sucking it. By now she had started to get loud.

I lifted my head for a second, never stopping what I was doing with my fingers. "Baby, you have to quiet down some the boys are awake."

"Shit…Tre…I can't! Damn…baby, you know exactly what

to do with this pussy." She moaned still grinding her pussy on my fingers and trying to get as much of them inside of her as possible. "Baby, stop talking and use your mouth to make me cum."

I gave her what she wanted. I put my head back between her thighs where I'd just come from and gave her clit a fit with my hurricane tongue! Her legs started shaking and she was cumming and hollering out my name. She grabbed the pillow and placed it over her head trying to muffle her screams.

I heard little footsteps running down the hall. Then they were trying to open the door. "What's wrong with ma? Is she okay? Daddy!" Shaun yelled.

"Yeah is she okay?" Quan added.

"Yeah your mama's fine. She hit her toe that's all!" I lied as I watched Kisha's body spasm from the powerful orgasm that I had just given her. "Go back and watch TV or go play in your room." I told them.

"Okay." They replied in unison.

I moved the pillow out of the way and moved up so that I

could kiss her. We kissed passionately as I allowed her to taste her own juices that were on my lips and tongue. She wrapped her legs tightly around my waist and her arms around my neck. "I love you so much Tre and after all that we have been through I am still very much in love with you."

"I love you too baby and after all of these years I am still very much in love with you also." I kissed her again and then got up and went into the bathroom and turned on the shower. I was getting undressed to step in when Kisha came in. She grabbed a wash cloth, wet it and put some soap on it and started to clean herself up at the sink.

"What are you about to do?" She asked as I stepped inside the shower and slid the glass door closed.

"I'm going to take a bath and then run over to Casper's crib for a lil while. Why?" I yelled over the sound of the water. I knew the bullshit was about to come.

"I just asked." I could hear the attitude in her tone. "Why you always gotta go over there for? I mean…damn, you act like every time you get a day off you gotta go somewhere instead of sitting here kickin it with me and your kids!"

That was the shit that got on my fuckin nerves right there! A nigga always had to hear some damn lip whenever he got ready to leave. I felt like if I work all week and take care of home I should be able to go out and kick it with the fellas for a little while without having to hear a lot of lip.

"Look, don't start that shit! I said that I was going over there for a lil while not all damn night!"

"Whatever!" She left out of the bathroom slamming the door behind her. Shit like that made me want to put my foot in her ass! I hated when she was nagging as hell.

I showered and then got dressed in a pair of red Nike sweats, a white tee and a pair of red/white Jordans. When I was done getting dressed I brushed my hair and slipped on my red VA fitted. I walked down the hallway and into the living room. Kisha was on the phone and the boys were sitting on the floor playing their X-box. I walked over to Kisha and tried to kiss her on the cheek but she moved so that I couldn't and smacked her lips.

"Stop acting stupid!" I snapped.

"Why don't you just go ahead wherever you are going?" She snapped right back.

"Man whatever. I ain't got time for this bullshit right here." I walked over and told my lil men to be good and that I would be back in a lil while. Then I was out.

When I got to Casper's crib I saw a few vehicles parked in the yard that belonged to some of my other homies. I already knew that them niggas was up in there drinking, gambling and getting blazed. I parked and then walked up on the porch and rang the doorbell. A few seconds later Casper's girl Tamika answered the door. She was a brown skinned chic with a long dark brown wavy weave that stopped midway her back. She was slim but curvy, probably about 5'7. She was cute but the bitch was a straight up hoe!

"Hey Tre…" She greeted her eyes roaming all over me and then finally landing back on my face. This bitch wasn't shit! I don't even know why Casper was fucking with her. She had fucked three of the niggas that we hung with and now he had her sorry ass staying up in his crib! I knew that she wanted to give me the pussy but truth be told. I wouldn't fuck her nasty ass with somebody else's dick!

"What's good? Where Casper'em at?" I asked already walking in.

"They all down in the basement." She said not bothering to move back out of the way so that I could get past her. I brushed right past her not paying her trifling ass any attention. I wasn't no slow nigga I knew what time it was. Yeah I fucked around but I did have standards and her dirty ass didn't meet them!

Lala

A week had gone by and I wasn't feeling any better. Nita was

so excited to have me here. She lived alone except for her three

year old daughter Maya, whom was one of the cutest little spoiled

babies that I had ever laid eyes on. Her and Maya's father, Jesse,

split up over two years ago and didn't have any dealings with one

another. She told me the reason was because she had come home

from work and caught him in bed with not one but two women

whom she later found out were prostitutes. She said that after she'd

caught him, he told her that he had a sex addiction but of course

she wasn't buying that bullshit.

At the time when she'd first told me I didn't either but that

was before I met Tre. Now I was beginning to think that the shit

just might be possible because I sure as hell had an addiction to the

bomb ass sex that I'd been getting for the past two years. For the

past week I had been going through withdrawals! I mean it was so

bad that I was tempted to go online and see if there were any rehabilitation centers close by for bitches that were addicted to good dick. I would've been up in there with the quickness sitting in the circle and when my turn came to introduce myself I would've stood up proudly and announced.

"Hello my name is LaQuela Chambers and I am addicted to good dick but not just any dick, the one that is attached to Tremaine Jefferson." There would've been no shame in my game!

I moped down the stairs. Nita was sitting on the sofa watching The Game. I didn't see Maya so I assumed that her little behind was still in bed. I spoke to Nita and then went over and sat in the huge bay window and looked out at the rain. I didn't feel like watching TV. I was too depressed.

Nita looked over at me. "How are you this morning?" She asked and then said. "I really don't even have to ask because it is written all over your face."

"I'm good." I mumbled unconvincingly, hoping that she wouldn't start with me. I wasn't in the mood for no damn lecture. I rested my head against the window seal and looked back out at the rain.

"No you're not!" She sucked her teeth. "You're sitting over there still thinking about that boy. Lala, I know that you don't want to hear what I am about to say but…"

"Well then don't say it!" I snapped. Why couldn't she just mind her fucking business? I knew that I was in her crib but that didn't automatically give her the right to preach to me every minute of every day.

"Yes, I am because I am your cousin and your best friend. If I don't keep it real with you, then who will?" She asked. "You knew from day one when you decided to lay with that man that he had someone and that he wasn't yours! You are just getting what you deserve! Haven't you ever heard the saying that everything that looks good to you ain't always good for you? Now when you called me and told me about you and this guy I warned you that you were playing with fire but noooo you was like 'Nita, I know that it ain't right but you just don't understand how he makes me feel!' You were thinking with your pussy and not your head! Now look at how he making you feel! All lost and depressed! Guess what though, I bet he's at *home* making his babymama feel like you wish you were feeling right now!" She rolled her eyes after she was done flapping her fuckin lips!

Ain't it a bitch how you can know that someone is telling you some shit that is right but you still don't want to hear that shit! I knew that she was right but the deed was done now. I couldn't take it back! Honestly I wouldn't take it back! I didn't regret any of it except for the fact that I had allowed my fuckin emotions to get involved!

"Whatever!" I got up from the window and stomped back upstairs to the guest room and closed the door. I laid across the bed on my back and stared up at the ceiling as the tears rolled from the corners of my eyes. I didn't even bother to wipe them. What for? More were guaranteed to fall. I laid there listening to the rain fall, it was pouring down outside. We were getting the wind and ran from a hurricane. My mind drifted back to the day when I first laid eyes on Tre.

I worked for a company called Service Master. We cleaned up office buildings after hours. We worked from five in the afternoon until we cleaned the last building. We worked all over the Tidewater area, for the past few months I had been working by myself. Sometimes I wouldn't get home until after three in the morning. One Tuesday afternoon my supervisor called me to inform me that he had hired a new guy and that he would be working with me. I was glad because I could get done quicker now and have some company as I drove from place to place.

That evening when I pulled into the parking lot of Service Master, I gathered my things from my car that I would need and locked it because I always drove the company van during work hours, they supplied the gas. I walked into the building and went straight to my supervisor's office as he had instructed me to do once I got to work. I walked in and saw a young dark skinned slim brother sitting in one of the leather chairs across from Mr. Johnson. They were engaged in a conversation when I walked in.

"Good evening Mr. Johnson." I greeted my supervisor. I

turned to the young gentleman that was sitting in the chair and extended my hand to him. "Hello, I'm Lala."

He stood and shook my hand. "Nice to meet you Ms. Lala. I'm Tremaine but everybody calls me Tre."

He was tall probably about 6'1, he had dark brown eyes, a close cut with thin side burns that connected to his goat-tee. He was wearing a white tee, a pair of baggy black sweats and a pair of black Tims on his feet. He was really nice looking but I had a feeling that he was going to get on my nerves because he was so young and probably would want to play around and not really take the job seriously. I'd worked with a few of them before and was not eager to work with another.

"Lala as I told you on the phone earlier. You and Tre will be working together. Just kind of show him the ropes and I'm sure he will get the hang of everything pretty quickly." Mr. Johnson said to me.

"Okay." I looked at Tre. "Are you ready to go?"

"Yes ma'am." He said while looking down at his phone, I

assume sending a text. When he stood I noticed his pants sagging off his ass. I shook my head because I was so damn sick and tired of seeing young guys walking around with their pants sagging, having to literally walk and try to hold them up.

"Okay then let's go." I walked out ahead of him ready to get the day started and get rid of him and soon as possible.

We hopped in the van. I strapped on my seatbelt while Tre sat his backpack on the floor and then reclined his seat before putting in his earphones so that he could listen to his ipod.

"Ummm…do you want to make that seatbelt click sir?" I asked as I waited for him to fasten his seatbelt.

He must not have heard me because he continued to sing the lyrics to Lil' Wayne's Lollipop. "*Call me so I can make it juicy for ya. Call me so I can make it juicy for ya. Shawty wanna thug bottles in the club…*"

"Tre!" I called loud enough so that he could hear me over the music.

He removed his earphones. "Yes ma'am Ms. Lala." The way

that my name rolled off his tongue should've been illegal. He was staring at me waiting for me to tell him why I'd called his name.

"Um…could you buckle your um…seatbelt?" I asked before redirecting my eyes straight ahead.

"Oh yeah sure. No problem." He sat his seat up some and buckled his seatbelt. "Is that better?" He asked flashing a perfect smile.

"Yep." I started up the van and pulled out of the parking lot and we headed to Chesapeake, VA for our first job. On the drive there I had the radio turned to 95.7 listening to all of my jams old and new skool. I was singing to the music, snapping my fingers and dancing. This was what I did on a daily basis as I drove to each location. I was so into it that I had forgotten Tre was even in the van until I noticed him watching me.

Embarrassed I laughed and said. "My bad."

"Oh you are good, I was enjoying the show. You can sing a lil bit and you got some sexy little moves. I especially like the lil move you do when you are windin' your midsection real slow…mmm. You ain't gettin' no complaints from over here." He said smiling and licking his lips.

Damn he was direct! He didn't even know me like that. "Excuse me? Are you always this straight forward?"

"Yep. I say whatever is on my mind. Why not?" He asked. I didn't respond because I actually didn't know what to say. I turned my attention back on the road.

"How old are you Lala?" he asked. I guess he'd gotten a little more comfortable because all of a sudden I wasn't Ms. Lala anymore I was just plain ol' Lala.

"I'm twenty-six about to be twenty-seven. And you?"

"Twenty-one about to be twenty-two." he said mockingly.

"Are you trying to be funny?"

"Who me? Nah never." We both laughed. He was turning out to be cool. I was starting to see that I may have been wrong about him.

During the next few weeks we became pretty good friends. We even exchanged numbers, it was innocent at first but I soon learned that may have been my first mistake because then we were texting each other even when we weren't working. Nothing out of the way just general convo. I was well aware of the fact that he had someone and that they had been together at that time for over five years. Little by little things started to escalate to another level between us. Tre was a huge flirt and I won't lie I enjoyed the attention and flirted right back. Not thinking anything of it until one night when we were cleaning our last office building.

I was bent over cleaning the bottom of the glass door, when Tre came up behind me and purposely bumped me from behind. "Excuse me Lala. I'm trying to clean the top of the glass for you because I know that you can't reach it." He said with his crotch still pressed firmly against my round backside.

"Well why don't you just clean the other one while I do this one?" I asked not bothering to move from the position that we were in.

"Because I'd much rather *do* this one." He said pressing against my backside a little more. He dropped the paper towels and glass cleaner that he'd been holding and placed his hands on my hips as he slowly grinded his crotch against my ass.

I felt myself becoming aroused. "Tre, as good as this feels I don't think that it would be a good idea." I said standing straight up.

He walked me up against the door and placed both of my hands against the glass with his hands over top of mine. "Why wouldn't it be a good idea?" He asked nibbling on my ear. His warm mouth on my skin cause my pussy to immediately juice up. "Ain't nobody here but the two of us and so there for we are the only ones who will know."

"Tre." I said my breathing pattern starting to change. This young ass nigga had my pussy doing jumping jacks! "You have someone and honestly I am not looking for anyone. Not only that but you are too young for me."

"Number one, I am aware of the fact that I have someone, you let me worry about that. Number two, I'm not trying to be your man, I'm just trying to make you feel good. You and I both are well aware of the sexual tension between the two of us. And number three my age ain't got shit to do with nothing. I promise you that if you give me this pussy I will have your ass up in her climbing the walls! I have bedded woman much older than you and trust me they are still blowing a nigga's phone up begging me to come and break them off."

I turned around to face him. "We can't do this." I tried to move but he wouldn't let me.

"Why not? You know that you want to. Look at how hard your nipples are." He said looking down at them nearly poking a hole through my shirt and bra. "How long are you going to be able to fight it, huh? We work together and I am not quitting anytime soon and I assume that you aren't either."

He did have a point but I still stuck to my guns. "I don't know but my answer is still no."

"Okay. I'm not about to beg for it but before it is all said and done you will be begging me to put out that fire that I've already ignited between your legs. I'm willing to bet that your pussy is so wet right now I could use your panties for a slip and slide." He said backing up some and then bending down to pick up the window cleaner and paper towels. He went over and began cleaning the other glass door while I finish the one that I had been working on.

The rest of the night I couldn't keep my mind off of the things that he'd said to me. He'd sure as hell hit the nail on the head. I did want him and I wanted him bad. I wanted to feel him inside of me in the worst way. It'd been over a year and a half since I'd had some real dick. I say real because I'd had plenty of artificial dick. My body was long overdue for some good loving.

That night when I made it home, I kicked off my shoes and stripped out of my clothes as soon as I made it through the front door. I nearly ran down the hallway to my bedroom. I reached in the nightstand beside my bed and grabbed my nine inch vibrator. I turned it on and laid back on my bed. I didn't have any time for playing. I needed some relief immediately. I placed the tip of my battery operated boyfriend directly on my clit and no sooner than it made contact I began to cum. When I'd gotten myself together I took the time to caress my breasts and play with my nipples while I stroked my toy in and out of my dripping wet pussy. I was so wet that I could feel my juices dripping down my ass cheeks. I closed my eyes and imagined that it was Tre playing with my breasts and fucking me nice and slow, allowing me to savor the feeling of him being inside of me. As those images flashed through my head I came long and hard.

That became a nightly routine for me. Tre would get me so worked up at work that by the time I made it home I had to immediately go to my bedroom and relieve myself. Sometimes I would just get myself off right there in the living room on the sofa. Tre was making it nearly impossible for me to continue to say no to him and fight off his advances. Even after he sent a picture of his thick long piece of equipment to my phone I still tried to resist but it was getting harder and harder. I used my vibrator so much that I ended up breaking it!

After weeks of saying no, I finally gave in. It was a Thursday night, I'd finished everything that I had to do. I was sitting on top of a desk waiting for him to finish vacuuming the floor so that we could leave work. I was listening to my ipod and singing along to Keith Sweat's How Deep Is Your Love. I had my eyes closed and was having dirty thoughts about Tre when I felt his lips on my neck. I thought that my mind was playing tricks on me. My eyes immediately popped open. He'd positioned his self between my legs and was planting kisses on my neck. His hands were like those of an octopus, they were roaming all over my body.

"What are you doing?" I moaned while holding onto the desk to brace myself.

"I thought you were singing to me asking how deep my love was. I'm trying to show you." He said making his way down to my breasts. I was wearing a low cut shirt that exposed the top of my breasts. He kissed my exposed cleavage and sucked on it leaving passion marks along the way.

"Tre…Tre please stop." I moaned not trying to push him away. I was tired of trying to resist him and acting like I didn't want him to blow my back out when in reality I knew that was exactly what I wanted. He took his fingers and traced circles around my nipples through my shirt. "Oh shit!" I squealed locking my legs around his waist. He dipped his head lower and started biting my nipple through my shirt. My nipples were extremely sensitive, I believe more sensitive than most women and him biting them nearly sent me through the roof! I snatched my earphones from my ears and tried to place them and my ipod on the table but they both fell to the floor. "Let's fuck I don't give a damn about age or anything else at this moment!"

He stopped assaulting my nipples for a moment to say. "Nah, I'm too young for you and I have a woman at home. This just wouldn't be a good idea." He said with a smirk before he went back to biting on my nipples through my shirt.

"Tre, don't fucking play with me!" I warned I was so turned on that I was willing to take it at this point! I was ready to feel him inside of me. Fuck all that bullshit that he was talking.

"No Lala! No means no!" He laughed.

"Tre, I am not playing with you!" I said tugging his shirt over his head revealing his slim but muscular tatted up body. That shit turned me on even more. I had a thing for niggas that were tatted up.

He walked over turned off the lights and then back over to me. He pulled my shirt over my head and then unsnapped my bra, freeing my full breasts. "Stand up." He instructed. I did as he said. He unfastened my belt and unsnapped my jeans and slid them down along with my panties. I kicked off my shoes and stepped out of my jeans and my panties, while he undressed. He picked me up, surprising me with how strong he was and sat me back up on the desk.

He went back to work on my breasts sucking them and biting them. With one of his hands he inserted two fingers inside of my pussy and began working them in and out of me. I hadn't had any in a while and my body was in desperate need of what he was giving it. He removed the two fingers that he'd been using to play in my pussy and held them up to my lips for me to taste my juices. I gladly took his fingers in my mouth and sucked them clean. He put them back inside of me and continued to finger my pussy. Then he pulled them out and began moving them back and forth over my clit.

"Damn Tre you are going to make me cum." I panted.

"I sure am over and over again. Go ahead and cum on my fingers baby. Let that shit go." He tried to kiss me but I turned my head.

"Nah-uh no kissing. That's how people catch feelings."

He laughed. "Okay, I can respect that." He started back sucking on my nipples as he continued to play with my clit. "Go ahead and cum for me."

His wish was my command. I skeeted all over his fingers. I thought that he was going to give me a chance to recover but I was wrong. He laid me back and entered me to the hilt. I could feel him stretching me open to accommodate his size. It hurt so good and when he started to move in and out of me and play with my clit I thought that I was going to lose my mind. I locked my legs tightly around his waist and road him until I came again. The only noise that could be heard throughout the entire office was the sounds of our pleasure filled moans and the slapping of skin.

After I came for the second time he pulled out of me and asked me to stand up and turn around so that he could hit it from the back. When I could feel my legs again I stood and turned around and bent over the desk. He lifted one of my legs up on the desk and entered me from behind. This time it wasn't a slow pace but instead he fucked me without mercy as he slapped my ass and made me yell out shit and beg for him to go harder and deeper. He was enjoying how my pussy was feeling and I knew it because of all of the noises he was making. When he was ready to come he pulled out and shot his load all over my ass cheeks. We were both silent for a while before Tre broke the silence by saying.

"Damn girl you got some good ass pussy! Oh we are officially cuddy buddies because I have to get some more of this!" And that right there was the beginning of my Tre addiction because after that we got it in on the regular.

Tre

Monday evening came entirely too fast. I was headed out the door and on my way to work. I kissed Kisha and told my two little men that I would see them later and to be good for their mama. Then I was out the door. I jumped inside my cream colored 2010 Dodge Charger. No sooner than I was out of the driveway my phone started ringing. I looked at the screen and saw Casper's name flashing on it. I pressed the send button and answered.

"What's good my nigga?" I answered.

"Ain't shit. Just hollerin' at you. You on your way to work ain't you?" He asked.

"Yeah man." My phone beeped alerting that I had another call. I took the phone from my ear and looked at the screen. I saw that it was Lala. "Aye let me hit you back my nigga. I have another call."

"Alright man do that."

I clicked over. "Hello."

There was a brief silence before she spoke. "Hey."

"Oh so you finally decided to call me and let me know that you were okay?" I snapped. "What kind of bullshit are you on?"

"I'm not on any kind of bullshit! I just didn't call because to be honest I didn't know what to say." She explained but it sounded like bullshit to me.

"How about calling and letting a nigga know that your ass is okay? That is some simple shit right there!"

"Tre, I didn't call to argue with you." She sounded sad. "I just called to let you know that I am fine. I know the way that I did everything wasn't exactly cool but I did what I felt like needed to be done at the time. I never have caused you any problems in all of the time that the two of us have been dealing with each other and I didn't want to start now. Can you understand that?"

Regardless of how upset that I was with her for not calling me sooner to let me know how she was doing. I couldn't do anything but respect the fact that she had chosen to walk away from our situation rather than cause drama like most bitches would have.

"Yeah, I understand that but I just felt like the two of us were better than this. You could've at least told me what the deal was. You didn't even give me the opportunity to properly say good-bye to you. I mean after dealing with somebody for two years you do develop some type of feelings for them. Even though I love my babymama, I do care about you too."

"I feel what you are saying but I just felt like this way was easier for me. I hadn't planned on telling you that I had caught feelings but when you called me the other day it all just came out." She paused for a moment and then continued. "I couldn't keep living there in Boykins, Tre. I think me moving was the best thing for us both."

She seemed to have everything figured out. "Well, I wish you the best."

"Thank you."

"No problem." I didn't feel like there was anything else to be said. "Well, I am almost at work so I am going to get off of this phone."

"Alright then, bye."

We hung up and I turned up the radio. As if someone was playing a cruel ass trick on a nigga, Secret Lover's was playing. I laughed out loud. "Ain't this some shit?" I turned off the radio and drove to work in silence, just me and my thoughts. I couldn't help but think about how sad Lala had sounded on the phone. Her mouth had been saying that she was fine but I could hear in her voice that she really wasn't. There was nothing that I could do though to change what had already been done. She was gone now and even though I didn't want her to go. I completely agreed that it was more than likely for the best. I wasn't willing to lose my family for anybody.

I pulled into the parking lot of Service Master and parked my car. I got my backpack out of the back which contained the things that I carried with me daily, like my music food, drinks, etc. I got out and locked up my car and went inside to see where I would be working that day.

"Hey Mr. Johnson." I greeted my supervisor as I walked into his office. He was a short heavy Caucasian man. He looked to be in his late fifties.

"How's it going Tre?" He asked scratching the bald spot in the top of his head.

"It's going alright. I can't complain. How about yourself?"

"I'm breathing so I guess I can't complain either." He laughed and coughed at the same time. "This cold is trying to get me down that's the only complaint I have."

"You'd better take something for that." I wasn't trying to stand around and small talk with him all day. "Where am I headed today?"

He looked down at the schedule on his desk. "I need you in Suffolk today. There are two buildings over there that I need you to take care of. Do you think that you think that you can handle that?"

"Yeah, I got it." He handed me a piece of paper with the names of the buildings and the addresses. I took the paper, folded it and put it in my pocket. "Alright then, I guess I'd better be getting on out of here. I'll talk to you later." I turned to walk out.

"Lala sure is missing. I'll tell you the truth. I miss seeing her come in here every day. She has such a great personality, always laughing and joking."

"Yeah, she is missing but I guess she had to do what she had to do."

"Yeah, I guess you're right. Did she say anything to you about why she was leaving? I'm not trying to be all up in her business or anything but was it financial reasons? I mean, I would've given her a raise or more hours if she'd just come to me and talked to me."

"Nah, she didn't say anything to me." I lied. "All she told me is that she was leaving."

"Hmmm…well I wish her the best. She seems like a nice young lady. She's going to make some gentleman very happy one day."

I didn't even want to begin to think about Lala fucking with another nigga. "Alright then, I'm going on and get started on these buildings."

"Alright then Tre, drive careful and I'll talk to you tomorrow."

That afternoon as I worked I thought about a lot of things. Mainly I thought about Lala. I couldn't understand why I was allowing her leaving to bother me so much. I kept getting a feeling that there was more to it than she was telling me. I couldn't quite put my finger on it but something just wasn't right. For her to pack up just out of the blue and leave like that just wasn't making any sense. It wasn't like she had just discovered overnight that she had feelings for me. She had to have known for a while now that she was feeling this way. She was hiding something! She'd probably met some nigga and went running to Danville to lay up with him! Bitches… She could've just kept it real with me and told me what the deal was instead of feeding me some bullshit ass story about leaving because she had developed feelings for me.

I'd become a little upset thinking about Lala. I decided to push all thoughts of her lying ass out of my mind. I turned up the volume on my ipod and grooved to DMX as I did my work. I didn't finish the last building until a little after two.

As I drove back to Service Master to pick up my car, Lala invaded my thoughts again. Damn this van brought back so many memories. The first time that I'd tasted her was in the back of this same van. I thought back to that night.

We had just finished cleaning our last office and were on our way back to the van. At this time we had been messing around for well over six months.

"I have a taste for some pancakes with strawberries and whipped cream. Mmmm that would be so good." She said as we walked to the back of the van to put our cleaning supplies in.

I opened up the back doors and she put in her things and then I put mine in. When she turned around I wrapped my arms around her waist. "I have a taste for some chocolate cream pie." I said suggestively.

"Tre all you think about sex! Goodness boy get your mind out of the gutter for two seconds!" She laughed.

"You wasn't saying that last night when I had you bent over touching your toes. You were saying, 'Oh my goodness Tre fuck me harder. Oh baby I love this dick!" I imitated her.

"Shut up!" She said hitting me playfully on the arm. "Move so that we can go to Ihop and I can get me some pancakes."

I still didn't move. "Under one condition."

"Tre, you are not getting any so move!" She said trying to get past me.

"I just wanna taste it. That is the only thing that you won't let me do. Why?"

"I just don't really care for oral sex. It doesn't do anything for me." She said screwing up her face.

"Hmmm, I tell you what. Give me one minute. If you don't like it I promise I will stop and we will go to Ihop and I will buy you some strawberry pancakes. But…if you give me one minute and you like it, we can still go to Ihop but you have to buy me some pancakes and give me some head but I want my head first!"

"What? Boy get out of my way! I am not buying you jack and I am not giving you any head...well not tonight anyways." She smiled at me. It was kind of chilly outside and her nose had turned red.

"You're right, I can understand if you are scared."

"Is that the best you can do at reverse psychology? If so you suck!" She giggled.

"I will suck something else if you stop acting all scared and let me." I said palming both of her ass cheeks. I knew how to get her. I started nibbling on her ear.

"Uh-uhh hell no! Stop it!" She tried to push me away but I held on to her tighter while licking on her ear and her neck. I truly could not get enough of her. Her entire body was my playground and I loved every inch of it. Don't get me wrong I enjoyed making love to Kisha but our lovemaking didn't have shit on how I felt when I was sexing Lala. The pleasure that she gave me was indescribable.

"Come on baby just one minute." I wasn't giving up easily.

"Tre we are in a parking lot and in case you can't feel it's cold out here!" I don't see how she could feel the cold with the way that she was bundled up. She had on gloves, a thick ass winter coat and a stocking cap!

"Shit, I know that's why I am trying to heat you up! If you stop trying to play all hard! I promise I will have you thinking that it's summertime out this motherfucka!" I was very confident in my head game and I knew that I would have her body temp at a 100 degrees or better. She knew it too but she just wanted to hear a nigga beg.

She laughed at me. "You are so damn cocky." She said caressing the side of my face with her glove covered hand. "Damn you make me sick because you know that I can't say no to your sexy ass. Come on…one minute that's it."

"One minute." I promised but come on, we both knew that this wasn't about to be no damn one minute once I got her out of them tight ass pants that she was wearing.

She climbed into the back of the van and I climbed in behind her. "You got me out here fuckin' in the back of the company van like I'm some hot in the ass sixteen year old."

"No baby, you're a hot in the ass twenty-seven year old." I laughed as I helped her out of her shoes, pants and panties.

"Whatever! You have one minute because I told you that I don't like oral sex. I just don't get any pleasure out of it." She went on and on.

"Lala will you please be quiet and let me do me?" I asked as I planted kisses up her thigh starting from the outside and working my way to the inside. I felt her legs start to tremble. "Damn baby, you coming already? I haven't even made it to your pussy yet." I teased.

"No, I told you that I was cold." She whined.

I didn't respond I just speeded up the process a little. I spread her thighs a little bit more and then I spread her lips with my fingers before flattening out my tongue and licking the entire length of her pussy. I did this a few times before I zone in on here clit. I flicked my tongue back and forth across it. I felt her trying to scoot back some. I tighten my arms around her thighs and pulled her back to me. I flicked and sucked and flicked and sucked until I had her trying everything in her power to get away from my tongue. I decided to fuck with her when I knew that I had her right on the verge of cumming. I let go of her thighs and said. "I'm done."

"Done?" She asked panting. "What do you mean? I was just about to cum." She was reaching for me trying to get me to go back where I had just come from.

"Lala, I'm sure that I heard you yelling stop. And I am positive that I heard you say that you didn't get any enjoyment out of oral sex." I was wiping her juices from around my mouth with my hand.

"Boy, I am gonna ask you to learn when and when not to play because right now is not the time! Now finish what you started!" She demanded.

I laughed at her. "Ummm…you know that I won right?" I teased.

She didn't respond she just pushed my head back between her thighs and I got her off twice before I stopped. I enjoyed all of the little sex games that we played.

When we were done I helped her get dressed and then we got in the van and headed to Ihop. On the way there I looked over at her and said. "You can pay off your debt this Sunday when I come over to your house for Sunday dinner."

"I got you." She smiled. "Just as long as you are willing to return the favor." We both burst into laughter.

I smiled at that memory, thinking to myself that we'd had some good times together. Then just as quick the feeling that she was lying to me returned.

By the time that I made it home that morning it was 3:30am, Kisha was sitting up on the sofa watching TV and eating grapes.

"Hey baby." she greeted me when I came in.

"Hey baby." I sat down my backpack and then walked over

and collapsed on the sofa beside her. She leaned over and kissed me. "What are you doing up so late?"

"I couldn't sleep so I decided to sit out here in the living room and watch some TV." She responded while trying to feed me a grape.

I opened my mouth and allowed her to feed it to me. I had a beautiful woman right here who loved me to death. It was time to do right by her and work on trying to be faithful I owed her that much.

"Baby, I wanted to talk to you about something that has been on my mind." Kisha said turning off the TV and setting the bowl of grapes that she had been holding on the coffee table. She laid her head on my chest and stared up at me. She always did this when she wanted something.

"What is it boo? I knew that you weren't just up this late for no reason at all." I laughed at my babymama trying to be slick thinking that she could fool me. I had been with her for seven and a half years I knew her better than she knew herself.

"Okay here goes. We have been together for almost eight years now and I was thinking that maybe it's time that we make this official. I mean I'm not planning on going anywhere and I hope that you're not so why not get married?"

I looked at her like she had two heads. I was hoping that I'd heard her wrong. Marriage? Damn that shit had caught me totally off guard. I knew for a fact that I wasn't ready for that yet! "Damn bae, are you sure that you are ready to jump the broom?" That was the only thing that I could come up with, being put on the spot like that.

She sat up straight and looked at me. I knew then that I had said the wrong thing. "What do you mean am I sure? Hell yes, I am sure." She snapped, swiveling her neck, her red hair swaying from side to side. "What were you thinking? We are just going to shack up forever? Nah, I want more than that! I deserve more than that! I have laid down and brought two of your children into this world! I take care of my family and I am not out here ripping and running these streets like a lot of these young women! I have been faithful to you since day one and I have put up with more than a little bit of your bullshit! I believe that those are damn good reasons for you to put a ring on my finger!" She preached. I didn't say anything. I just sat there and allowed her get everything off her chest. "Don't just sit there looking crazy! Say something Tre!"

I ran my hand over my face. "I hope that you don't think you talking shit is going to make me do anything!" I said and ran my hand up her thigh, hoping to distract her. I needed to get her off this subject and quick because I knew that if I told her the truth we were just going to end up arguing for most of the night and I wasn't in the mood for that shit!

She hit my hand and removed it from her thigh. "Tre, I am serious! Stop trying to fuck and answer the question? Why can't we get married?"

I leaned my head back on the sofa and looked over at her. I knew that I had to try and chose my words carefully. "Kisha, I am not saying that we can't get married. You're already wifey...you know that."

She shook her head. "Fuck being wifey! I want to be the wife nigga! W-I-F-E!" She spelled it out as if I didn't know what she meant. "I want a ring and your last name!"

Instead of arguing with her I decided to tell her what she wanted to hear. It wasn't like I had to marry her the next day or anything. All she wanted to hear was that I would marry her. "Alright baby, yes we can get married."

Her face lit up like a Christmas tree and she dived over in my arms! "Awwww…I love you baby!" She squealed planting kisses all over my face and then finally on my lips. She straddled my lap and tongued me down real nice and slow. "Baby, I love you so much. I can't wait to become Mrs. Tremaine Jefferson."

"I love you too baby." I told her caressing her butt underneath her nightgown. I'd just made her the happiest woman on the face of the earth by telling her that we could get married. I felt kind of fucked up for lying but if I had said that I wasn't ready to get married she would've been ready to cut my ass. I wasn't in the mood for all of that tonight. Hopefully, I could just buy her an engagement ring to keep her happy for the time being and put off this marriage shit for at least another two years.

"Come on baby. Let's go to bed." Kisha said getting up from my lap and taking my hand.

I got up and followed her to the bedroom. We made love for the next hour and then she fell asleep in my arms shortly after. I couldn't sleep though. I had entirely too much shit on my mind to try and sleep. I just laid there staring up at the ceiling, my mind consumed by thoughts of Lala. I couldn't for the life of me understand why she was on my mind so heavy. Was it possible that my feelings for her were deeper than I had realized?

Kisha turned over and snuggled up closer to me. I looked over at her. *Damn she deserves better than this shit. Here I am laid up next to her thinking about another bitch! I've gotta get my shit together. Fuck Lala! I've gotta push her out of my head and move the fuck on. Kisha has had my back through thick and thin. It's time that I straighten the fuck up and do right by her.* I kissed Kisha on her forehead. *Yeah, fuck Lala! She's right, she did both of us a favor by leaving…*

Lala

I was up for the fourth morning in a row hovering over the toilet puking up my guts. I was now ten weeks pregnant and the morning sickness was kicking my ass. I'd known about the pregnancy now for three weeks. That was another reason why I'd moved. I hadn't told anyone about the pregnancy because I was still undecided as to whether or not I wanted to keep the baby. I really didn't believe in abortion but at the same time I didn't want to bring a child into the world and it not be able to have a relationship with its father. I felt like that wouldn't be fair to the child nor would it be fair to Tre. I felt like he deserved the right to know about the baby but I didn't know how to tell him. If I told him about this baby it would only open up a can of worms that I was not ready to deal with. I knew how strongly he felt about being a father and taking care of his children and in my heart I really felt like he would want to do the same for this baby but how could he?

He already had a family. I also knew that he wouldn't want Kisha or anyone else to ever find out about this baby. That would mean that my child would have to forever remain a secret. I was so confused about what I should do. I still had a little time before I had to make a definite decision.

I flushed the toilet and then washed my face and brushed my teeth before going downstairs to get me some water. Nita was downstairs when I got down there. She was sitting at the table eating some Oreos and having a glass of milk with them.

"Good morning Nita." I greeted her sounding like shit. I walked over to the refrigerator and got out a bottled water and drank most of it before taking it from my lips.

"Good morning." She looked at me strangely. "Are you okay? You don't look too good."

"Nah, I'm not." I sat down at the table and held my head in my hands. Tears rolled down my face. I needed to talk to someone. Carrying all of this shit around on the inside was killing me. I felt like I was about to lose my mind.

"What's wrong? You know that you can talk to me about anything. Even if I don't agree with whatever it is. I am still going to be here for you." I wiped my face with my hand. She got up from the table and got me a paper towel and handed it to me. "Here you go."

"Thank you." I took the paper towel and wiped my face. She went back over to her chair and sat back down. "I'm pregnant." I blurted. There it was out there in the open!

"I had a feeling of that. Do you know how far along you are?"

"I don't really know. I took a home pregnancy test three weeks ago. My period was already a month late when I took the test." I replied before breaking down and sobbing loudly. "Nita, I don't know what to do! I don't want to kill my baby but what other choice do I have?"

"Stop that crying first of all! That isn't good for you or that baby." She instructed. "Now does Tre know?"

"No, I didn't tell him." I replied between sobs.

"Why not? It is his baby isn't it?"

"Yes."

"Well he deserves the right to know."

I shook my head no! "I can't do that Nita. He already has a family."

"Shit that ain't nothing new! Both of y'all been knew he had a family when y'all started messing around! It didn't matter then obviously! What you plan on keeping this baby and raising it by yourself and not telling him about it?"

"I don't know." I mumbled.

"Well you need to start finding out!"

"I know but if I tell him I don't know what his reaction will be."

She held up her hand. "Hold up! Are you saying that you think he will be upset with you or try to deny it?"

"No, I'm not saying that at all. Tre isn't that kind of person. I'm just saying he may want me to get rid of it because I know he doesn't want his girl to find out and I am not sure if I want to get rid of it. Then again he may not ask me to get rid of it but of course I will have to keep my baby a secret. If I am going to have to keep it a secret anyways then I may as well raise it by myself and not tell him."

"Lord have mercy, Lala. Girl what were you thinking to be sleeping with this guy without using any protection or at least being on birth control?"

Why does she always have to sound like a fucking after school special? I thought to myself. "I was on the pill Nita I just forgot to take a few." I admitted.

"Okay so did you also forget to ask him to wrap up his pickle?" She looked at me and waited for an answer.

"Nah, I didn't forget we did use condoms a few times but it didn't feel as good."

She shook her head. "Lala, I don't know what has gotten into you. You use to be such a smart young woman."

"I still am a smart woman! I've just made a few dumb decisions. I'm not sitting over here saying that I am proud of all of the decisions that I've made but I also can't sit here and tell you that I regret it all either because then I would be lying! I'm human! I'm not the first nor the last woman to ever sleep with somebody else's man and get pregnant! So don't sit over there and try to look down on me like I am! I am talking to you because I need somebody right now and I thought that of all the people in the world you are the one person that I could talk to! I appreciate you keeping it real with me but damn!" I snapped. I loved my cousin to death but she was really starting to get on my nerves.

Nita let out a frustrated breath. "Listen it's not that I am trying to be a pain in your ass but honestly I just can't help thinking about his girlfriend. She doesn't deserve what the two of you have been doing to her behind her back! She is home taking care of his children thinking that he is out working to provide for his family but in reality he is somewhere laid up with you! That shit is really fucked up! I remember how I felt when I walked in and caught Ron with those two bitches! I felt like someone had ripped my heart clean out of my body! I look at you day in and day out walking around here crying and moping over somebody else's man! Are you fucking kidding me? For real for real you need your ass whooped!"

I gave her the look like no this heifer didn't. "Ummm…first and foremost if his babymama thinks she's bad enough to whoop my ass then she is more than welcome to come try it! Second of all what went down with Tre and I don't have shit to do with Ron fucking prostitutes in your home and in your bed! Yeah I know that what we were doing was wrong but I will say it again it is done now and I can't change it! How you gone try to talk shit to me because your man fucked up? That ain't got shit to do with me! You knew before I got here what the deal was because I had told you! If you felt like me being here was going to make you relive some old pain then you should've told me that I couldn't come! Not walk around here saying lil fly shit because you feeling some type of way about what Ron did! I didn't fuck Ron I fucked Tre! You talking about I used to be smart, well I am smart enough to know that you need to deal with the issues that you have with *your past* and stop taking that shit out on me! I can deal with you giving me advice and even giving me your opinion but not feeling like you can compare the two situations and say to me the shit that you really should be saying to Ron!" I stood to leave out of the kitchen.

"I am not taking shit out on you! I am just calling it the way that I see it! What makes you any better than them two bitches that was laid up in my bed with my man? Y'all are all the same breed! Bitches who go around sleeping with the next bitch's man because you can't find your own!" She was shouting now!

"Bitch fuck you! Let me share something with your stupid ass! In both situations no one was raped! I didn't rape Tre and those women didn't rape Ron! Hell in your situation that motherfucka was paying for pussy so you know that no one raped his ass! I may be wrong for sleeping with Tre but the truth of the matter is. I didn't have a commitment to anyone! He did! He knew that he had a woman at home but he still chose to deal with me! I didn't put a gun to his head! He was a willing participant! Bitches kill me all quick to blame the other woman like she raped the nigga

or something! I don't owe anybody shit at the end of the day! Hell.
If the shoe was on the other foot she probably would've did the
same thing to me and I couldn't blame anybody but my man! The
nigga that is supposed to be committed to me!"

"Yeah but you did lie down and spread your legs though!
Now look at you! Pregnant and crying the blues because you got to
hide your baby! His baby mama ain't got to hide hers though, now
do she? Nah, but that's what happens when you settle for being a
side bitch!"

I took a few steps closer to her. "You are going to say about
two more words and I am going to drop your ass right here in your
kitchen!" I was dead serious. She was about to catch the beat down
of her life! "I may be the side bitch and I may have to hide my
baby but you best believe with or without Tre me and mines is
going to always be okay! See the difference between me and most
side bitches and is that I have never had main bitch expectations!
I've always known my position! I don't expect Tre to run off into
the sunset with me! I knew from day one that would never happen!

Emotionally right now, yes I am catching hell but I have no one else to blame but me! I will be okay though because I'm not a weak bitch! This bitch right here can handle hers, you best believe that!"

"What are you trying to say?"

I looked her up and down and then in her eyes. "I am saying that regardless of the way shit is now I am going to pick up the pieces and move on. Not continue to live in the past and cry over spilled milk. Everything happens for a reason. This has happen to me for a reason. I plan to learn from it and make the best out of a bad situation. Like I said I am not the first to end up in this same situation and I won't be the last! It ain't about what I did...it's about what I do from this point on! Right now I am about to go upstairs and pack my shit so that I can leave your house before we end up fucking each other up! This living arrangement isn't working out!"

"Fine with me." She spat.

I walked out of the kitchen and left her standing there. I went upstairs and packed all of my things. I made several trips to my car, carrying my things out. Nita sat on the sofa watching. When I was done loading everything up in my car. I reached in my pocketbook and took out five hundred dollars. I handed the money to Nita. "Thank you for allowing me to stay here."

"I don't want your money." She rolled her eyes.

I dropped the money on the sofa next to her and walked out.

Tre

As the weeks rolled by I was able to pretty much push Lala out of my head. Not completely but for the most part and concentrate more on my relationship with Kisha. I was going to work and coming straight home, spending more time doing family stuff. I realized that all of the time that I'd been spending lying and making up excuses to slide off and kick it with Lala. I'd been missing out on a lot.

It was Thursday night and I'd cooked dinner so that Kisha could have a break. I'd cooked fried turkey chops, mashed potatoes, sweet peas and canned biscuits.

"This is good daddy." Shaun said chewing a mouthful of peas.

"Thanks lil man. Your daddy got a few skills in the kitchen." I bragged reaching over and rubbing my little man on the head.

"You still don't cook better than mama!" Quan added his two

cents.

"That's right baby." Kisha laughed and then looked at me and poked out her tongue. "You do alright but my baby knows who the real chef is!"

"Quan, how are you going to sit over there and hate on your daddy like that? You are supposed to be on my side. We men have to stick together." I joked. He shook his head no. "Boy what do you mean no?"

"He's a mama's boy!" Shaun teased.

"I think you're right Shaun." I played along.

"No, I'm not!" Quan pouted folding his arms.

"Is too!" Shaun kept taunting him.

"Maaaa…tell him to stop!" Quan whined.

Kisha reached over and popped Shaun hard on his arm! He let out a squeal and started to cry. "Stop teasing him!"

"Whoa…chill out!" I snapped. "He was only playing around! He didn't mean any harm. We were all just having fun!"

"It's not fun when you are making someone else feel bad!"

She snapped back!

"Kisha…for real?" I gave her a look that told her she was pissing me off! "It wasn't even that serious!"

"Well it was to Quan!"

I got up from the table and dumped my food in the trash! She'd caused me to lose my appetite. "Y'all boys finish up your food so that you can take your baths and then y'all can read me a book."

"Okay!" Quan replied smiling. They loved reading to me so that they could show me how well they were reading.

Shaun didn't say anything. He was slowly eating his food and sniffling. He wasn't crying anymore by now his little tears had dried on his face. "Stop looking so sad Shaun." I told him. "If you do a good job reading, I'll give you a popsicle before you go to bed."

That brought a smile to his face. I left out of the kitchen and went into the bedroom. I grabbed my laptop and sat down on the bed, propping some pillows behind my back and lying up against the headboard. I grabbed my cigarettes off of the nightstand and the lighter. I let lit one up and then powered up my laptop and logged in to Facebook. As I strolled down my newsfeeds I saw a status update from Lala. It said. *These past few weeks haven't been easy but with each day that goes by it gets better. Still missing home but I know that I made the right decision.*

I started to comment but then decided against it. I figured that it was best if I just kept things the way that they were. I stayed on Facebook a little while longer before logging out and browsing the web.

Kisha came into the bedroom. "So I guess you are mad now because I popped Shaun." Those were the first words out of her mouth.

"Don't come in here with that! If you came in here to start an argument then you need to take your ass right back in there!" She knew that she'd been dead wrong for how she had over reacted. She'd taken things to a whole other level for no reason at all.

"Who are you talking to like that?" She asked placing her

hand on her hip and tilting her head to the side causing a strand of her red hair to fall in her face. She removed her hair from her face and continued to stare at me waiting for an answer.

"Kisha go ahead." I warned.

"Why you acting like I abused him or something?"

I looked up at her. "I never said that you abused him but I do feel like you blew shit out of proportion! We were all joking around having a good time. He wasn't doing anything wrong! He was playing with Quan. You didn't have to hit him!"

She just stood there looking at me for a second like she was trying to think of something to say. Finally she let out a sigh and said. "Maybe I shouldn't have hit him but I didn't really approve of him teasing Quan like that after he'd asked him to stop."

"Kisha, all he said was that Quan was a mama's boy because he took your side instead of mines. Where is the harm in that? If I had felt like he was being mean to him I would've told him to stop." I let out a frustrated breath. "My thing is that we were all having a nice time and then that happened and ruined everything.

All you had to do was ask him to stop. That's it."

"Alright, I see your point. I guess I did over react a little but you know Quan is the more sensitive one so I am a little more protective over him."

I shook my head. "Well he is going to have to get out of that sensitive mess and toughen up! What he gone come home crying to you every time someone says something to him that he doesn't like?" I asked her but didn't wait for an answer. "I am raising little men not princesses!"

"Bae, he is only seven!"

"I am aware of that but he still isn't about to be around here crying and whining all the time! You need to stop babying him so much. Don't be making my son all soft and shit!"

She rolled her eyes. "Boy whatever!" She walked over and sat down on my lap. She kissed me, caressing my face. "Are we good now?"

I wrapped my arms around her and smacked her on her ass. "Yeah, we're good."

"I love you."

"I love you too."

She kissed me again. "Bae, I want you to know that I see the effort that you have been putting into our relationship lately and I want you to know that it is appreciated. You've been helping me out around the house more and spending more time with me and the boys. I don't know what has gotten into you but I like it."

I smiled, giving her thigh a light squeeze. "Nothing has gotten into me. I just love my family a lot and I want y'all to know it. I want you to know that even though I've done some fucked up things in the past. I appreciate you. You've stuck with my black ass when most women would've been packed their shit and left!"

"Yeah, we've been through a lot but every relationship has its ups and downs. You've taken me through a lot and there were times when I did think about packing my shit and leaving but I couldn't because I love you too much to walk away." A tear rolled down her cheek and I wiped it away with my finger. "I've had people tell me that I was stupid for staying with you and putting up with your cheating. Those people don't know what I feel in my heart for you. Those people don't know what I see when I look at you. They are on the outside looking in. They don't know that times when my family turned their backs on me. You were here. I remember that time when I had pneumonia and thought that I was going to leave this world. You stuck by my side and took care of me. I remember hearing you pray asking God to please make me better because you couldn't imagine having to live without me. It's those things that made me stick with you all of these years."

Her little speech left me speechless. It wasn't every day that we sat down and had a heart to heart. I knew that she loved me but hearing her break it down like this touched me in a special way. "Damn bae, you make a nigga want to let a few slide." I kissed her. "Damn girl."

She wiped her tears away and laughed. "Be quiet silly." She hit me playfully on the arm.

Quan and Shaun burst into the room. "We finished eating!" They both announced.

"Alright, well I am going to run your bath water. One of you can take a bath in mama and daddy's bathtub and the other one can take a bath in y'all tub." I told them.

"I want to take my bath in here." Quan replied.

"That's cool with me." I tapped Kisha and asked her to get up so that I could run the boys bath water.

"Well while you get them ready for their baths I am going to go in the living and finish reading my book." She left out of the room and I went into the bathroom and started running water in the tub for Quan. While his water was running I went across the hall and started Shaun's water.

"Y'all get you some underwear and your pajamas." I told the boys. They went and did as I had said.

After the boys were done with their baths, each of them read a book to me. They did such a good job that I gave them both a Popsicle and then we played for a little while before I put them both to bed. Once they were in bed, Kisha and I took a shower together and then went to bed.

Lala

I was laying down watching TV in my hotel room. I'd been
renting a room at the Innkeeper over on Piney Forest Rd. for the
past few weeks. I'd lucked up and gotten a housekeeping job here
the week before when one of the other housekeepers quit. I asked
the manager if I could have the job. He told me to fill out the
application and I did. When he saw that my previous job had been
one dealing with janitorial services he told me that he was sure that
I'd be great for the job and hired me right on the spot. Plus he gave
me a discount on my room. That allowed me to be saving most of
my paycheck. I was still putting in applications though because I
needed a part-time gig. I was also looking for a place. I'd put in
applications at most of the apartment complexes in the area. I was
hoping to hear something back from them soon. I was so glad that
I'd been saving my money and not blowing it like most young

people. My mama had always told me that you never know what might happen and you will need something to fall back on. That is why I tried to keep money in the bank and it had turned out to be a good thing.

I laid there on the bed watching some movie on Lifetime but I wasn't really into it. I was hungry and craving some tacos. I laid there debating on whether or not I was going to go out and get some or if I was just going to order a pizza instead. I really didn't feel like going out anywhere. I had become so lazy. All I wanted to do was lay around and sleep if I wasn't working. I had to literally make myself get out of bed and do stuff. I decided that I was going to put on some clothes and go out and get me some tacos. I'd been in bed all day. I needed to get out!

I got up, showered and got dressed in a pair of grey sweats, a black tee and my black forces. I went into the bathroom, took my scarf off and combed down my wrap. My hair was dark brown and shoulder length with blonde highlights. Since I'd been pregnant my hair had been growing like crazy! It was almost past my shoulders now. I brushed my teeth and put on a little bit of lip gloss. I looked in the mirror.

"That's good enough. I ain't trying to impress nobody."

I grabbed my coat, keys and my wallet and left out to go and get my food. I drove over to the Taco Bell on Riverside Dr. I decided to eat inside instead of ordering my food and going back to the room. I ordered six hard shell tacos and a sweet tea. Once I had my food I found a table towards the back next to a window. I sat down and started to eat my food. I looked out of the window and saw a young Caucasian couple getting out of the car. The young man was helping his pregnant girlfriend get out. He wrapped his arm around her as they walked inside. A wave of loneliness swept over me. I turned my attention back to my food but unconsciously my eyes wandered back to the couple who were now standing in line waiting to order. They looked so happy and in love. They laughed and giggled, whispering back and forth as they waited. He rubbed and caressed her stomach.

For some reason what Nita had said to me weeks ago when

we had gotten into it popped into my head. *"Now look at you! Pregnant and crying the blues because you got to hide your baby! His baby mama ain't got to hide hers though, now do she? Nah, but that's what happens when you settle for being a side bitch!"*

"I guess you were right about that part Nita." I mumbled getting up from the table and dumping the rest of my food into the garbage. My appetite was gone. I drove back to the room with thoughts of Tre heavy on my mind. I wanted to call him but I knew that I couldn't. He had probably moved on to the next chic and wasn't even thinking about my black ass. I went inside my room, undressed and got back in bed. I laid there trying to go to sleep for well over and hour but couldn't. Nita's words kept haunting me and Tre was so heavy on my brain that it was impossible for me to fall asleep.

I got up and put back on my tee shirt. I walked over and sat at the table that was in my room and powered on my laptop. I logged on to Facebook to see what was going on up there. It was the same as usual everybody telling all of their business. I shook my head.

I'd hidden Tre's post so that I couldn't see what he posted unless I went to his page. I decided to go on his page to see what he'd been up to. I hadn't checked since I'd left home. I typed in his name and clicked on his page. I saw that he'd uploaded some new photos of himself, Kisha and the boys. They looked extremely happy. I clicked on a photo of him and Kisha. He had his arms around her from behind as she stood in front of him smiling like she was the happiest woman in the world. Pains of jealousy and envy swept throughout my entire body. I went back to his page and strolled down reading his most recent status. *Focused on getting paper and taking care of my fam...fuck everything else! To all of you niggas that's got a good woman in your corner that holds you down, takes care of you and most importantly puts up with your bullshit, you'd better hold on to them. I'm damn sure holding on to mine! Shout out to my Queen Kisha...I love you woman!*

I felt like somebody had just punched me in the throat! I quickly logged off and closed my laptop. I sat there for a few minutes just trying to digest what I'd read. I realized one thing, it was time for me to forget about this man and focus on myself and this baby that I was carrying. There was no way in hell that I could ever let him know now about our baby. Honestly I couldn't see it doing anything but causing a lot of trouble that I didn't feel like dealing with.

I opened my computer back up and went back on Facebook. This time I deleted Tre from my page. It was time to delete him from my life and my thoughts but most importantly from my heart. I'd known from day one that he was already taken so there was no use in me waiting around like he was going to call me up and confess his undying love for me and beg me to come back. That wasn't going to happen.

My phone vibrated on the nightstand startling me. I jumped placing my hand over my chest. "Damn." I got up and went over and picked up my phone. There was a text message from my mom.

Mom: Hey baby, just checking on you to see if you are okay.

Me: Yes ma'am. I'm fine...about to go to bed. I love you.

Mom: Love you too. Call me tomorrow.

"Okay, I will."

I placed my phone back on the nightstand and got in bed. As much as I didn't want to think about the images of Tre and Kisha or his Facebook status that was all that I thought about until I fell asleep.

Lala

Over the next few weeks, all I did was work and save my

money. I'd set some goals for myself. The first thing was to find a

place within the next few months. I had to find a place before the

baby was born because there was no way in hell I was staying in a

hotel room with my baby. I'd also decided to write a book. I'd

already gotten started. The title of my book was Confessions Of A

Side Chic. The idea of course had come from my own personal

experience. I figured that writing about my situation would be sort

of therapeutic and if it turned out to be a good story I might could

try and get it published. I refused to sit around and cry over spilled

milk! I wasn't going to allow the bad choices that I'd made

determine the rest of my future! It wasn't the end of the world.

Millions of women raised kids by themselves every day and I

could do the same! I wanted to be someone that my baby could be proud of though. I didn't want the only story that people ever told my child was how I got knocked up by somebody else's man and ran away from my home to try and hide it! Hell no! My story was going to be different!

I sat in the doctor's office on Wednesday evening flipping through the pages of a Paula Dean's cooking magazine and waiting to be called to the back. This was my first doctor's appointment, I knew that I was about three months pregnant but I wasn't exactly sure. I felt bad that I hadn't gone to the doctor before now to make sure that my baby was okay. It was alright though because from here on out I was going to make sure that I was at every appointment to ensure that I delivered a healthy baby.

A young woman who looked to be in her late twenties or early thirties came in and took the seat next to me. Her stomach was way out there like she was about to pop at any second. "Hey." She spoke looking over at me with a warm smile. Her hair was in microbraids pulled up into and ponytail with some down in the back. She had skin the color of mocha, dark brown beady eyes and when she smiled I noticed the wide gap between her two front teeth. She was about 5'6 and very petite except for her baby bump.

"Hey. How are you?" I replied politely.

She let out a loud sigh and rubbed her stomach. "Tired." We both laughed. "Girl, my back and feet are killing me! I can't wait to drop this load! Only three more months!"

I looked at her huge belly. "Three?"

She laughed. "I know right! It looks like I am about ten months now!"

I shook my head and unconsciously rubbed my own belly, praying that I wouldn't be that big even at nine months. My belly had started to grow a little bit. "Gosh, I don't think you are going to make it another three months! Your stomach looks like it might pop at any second!"

"Yeah it does but I was big like this with my first son."

"Oh really? How old is your first son? I know he is excited about becoming a big brother!" I smiled.

I watched as a sad expression covered her face. "He was five.

He passed a few months ago."

"Oh my God!" My heart went out to this woman that I'd just met only a few minutes ago. I couldn't even imagine what she must've been going through on the inside. "I am so sorry for your loss. If you don't mind me asking, what happened?"

"Car accident…loss my son and my husband."

My hand went up to my chest. "Goodness, I am so sorry."

"Thank you." She smiled but it looked to be forced. "Is this your first one?" I could tell that she was trying to change the subject.

"Yes ma'am." I replied still feeling some type of way after hearing that she'd just lost her son and her husband.

She laughed. "Girl, how old do I look? You are over there talking about yes ma'am! I am only thirty years old!"

I laughed too. "I am so sorry. By the way I am LaQuela but you can call me Lala." I offered her my hand for her to shake.

She shook my hand. "I'm Denise but you can call me Nisey."

"Nice to meet you Nisey."

"Likewise." She replied. "Are you from here?"

"No, I have a cousin that lives out here. I just moved here almost two months ago…I needed a change."

"Hmph and you moved here?"

"Well it was kind of something that I had to do as opposed to something I wanted to do. I like it though. I just don't know anybody out here. My cousin and I had words right after I moved out here so I am pretty much alone."

"Oh I know how that can be. It's never easy dealing with family." She gave me a sympathetic look. "Do you have a cell?"

"Yeah."

"Tell you what. Program my number in your phone and that way you won't have to feel alone anymore." She said smiling. "I could use someone to talk to as well. Besides I am a firm believer that God places people in your path for a reason. He knew that you needed someone and so here I am."

I was starting to like this stranger. She seemed like a really nice person. I took out my cell and typed in her name. "What's your number?"

"434-555-0001."

I typed in the number and hit save. "Now don't get mad because I use it too much and be ducking my calls!" I joked.

She shook her head. "Oh honey you may end up feeling the same way about me." We chit chatted for a few more minutes, getting to know each other before the nurse came out and called me to the back.

I got up and grabbed my pocketbook. "Alright Nisey if I don't see you when I come out I will give you a call later. My number will show up as a 757 number."

"Okay. I hope that everything is okay with the baby."

"Thank you. I hope so too." I followed the nurse to the back.

"Hello Ms. Chambers. How are you today?" The older white nurse asked.

"I am doing quite fine and yourself?"

"I'm doing just great." We walked over to the scale. "Hand me your bag and then step up there so that I can get your weight." I did as instructed. "Okay…162. Alrighty, do you think you could step right in that restroom right over there and get me a urine sample. The cups are in the metal medicine cabinet right above the toilet. You can leave the cup on the counter next to the sink. Be careful not to knock it over and spill the urine. You'd be surprised at how many ladies do that." She said pointing to a door on the right. "I'll take your bag in the examination room which is right next door. Come in there when you're done."

"Okay…thanks." I went into the restroom and got down a cup and peed in it like she had asked. I sat the cup on the counter and washed my hands. Then I went into the examination room where the nurse was waiting for me.

She handed me a thin paper gown. "Here take this. Take off everything and put this on so that the opening is in the front. I am going to step out so that you can undress, then I'll be back." She left the room. I undressed, put on the gown and then folded my clothes into a neat pile and placed them in the chair that sat in the corner next to the window along with my pocketbook. I sat down on the examining table. A few minutes later there was a soft tap at the door.

"It's just me, Nurse Susan." The nurse said walking back into the room. She started to check my vitals and take my temperature. She wrote down everything as she went. "Your blood pressure looks good. That's a good thing. You don't want to suffer from high blood pressure. So many women develop it during pregnancy," I didn't say anything I just listened. "You have the most beautiful hazel green eyes. They aren't contacts are they?"

"No ma'am." I was used to people asking me that.

"They're beautiful."

"Thank you."

"Well I am going to step out. Dr. Porter should be in shortly." With that she was gone. I sat there looking around the room and waiting for Dr. Porter to come in.

A few minutes later a tall slim greying middle-aged black woman walked in. She had her hair pulled back into a bun. "Hello, I am Dr. Patrice Porter. How are you today?"

"I'm fine, thank you. I'm LaQuela Chambers."

"Nice to meet you, Ms. Chambers. When was your last period?"

"In December."

She looked like she was counting it up in her head. "Ooh that was three months ago. So you are at least three months along?"

"Yes, ma'am."

"You know it is very important that mothers get the proper prenatal care during pregnancy to ensure a healthy pregnancy as well as a healthy baby."

That made me feel like such a bad mother. I dropped my head. "Yes ma'am I know. I've just been going through a few things and just really getting settled here."

"I understand. Alright, let me examine you and then I am going to do and ultra sound and see just how far along you are." I grew excited at the mention of her doing an ultra sound! That meant that I was going to get to see my little one. She did her examination and then she let me hear the baby's heartbeat.

"Hmmm there it goes. Oh goodness, that little joker has a strong heartbeat!" She giggled.

The sound of my baby's heartbeat brought tears to my eyes. It also made me feel motivated more than ever to get my life in order. I had to do everything in my power to ensure that she or he had the best life possible since I had ruined the chances of my child having a real family.

The sound of Dr. Porter's voice interrupted my thoughts and brought me back to reality. "Okay let's see this little munchkin." She squeezed some cold gel on my stomach and then started to perform the ultrasound. The screen was facing her and so I couldn't see. The anticipation was killing me. "Oh boy…well isn't this something?'

"What? What's wrong?" I asked growing worried.

"Oh nothing's wrong doll baby but you are in for a bit of a surprise." She responded turning the monitor around so that I could see.

I looked at the monitor but couldn't make out what I was

looking at. "Ummm…I don't know what I'm looking at exactly." I admitted.

She let out a chuckle and pointed at the screen. "You are looking at 1 baby here and 1 baby here."

I was sure that I'd heard her wrong. "Say what?"

She repeated. "Here's one baby and here's the other. Ms. Chambers, you are fourteen weeks pregnant with twins." The room started to spin and I felt lightheaded. "Are you alright?"

I couldn't respond. I just laid there and cried.

Tre

It was Saturday and being that I had the weekend off I decided to kick it with the fellas. I hadn't kicked it with my boys in a minute. All of my time had been going into spending time with Kisha and the kids. Today was my day. I took a shower and got dressed in a pair of black Jordan sweats, a white tee, a pair of all black Jordans and a black VA fitted. I'd just gone to the barbershop that morning and gotten a fresh cut and shave. I looked myself over in the full length mirror in the bathroom one more time before going down the hall into the living room.

Kisha was sitting on the sofa with her head stuck in a book as usual. "Alright sexy, I'll be back in a few." I kissed her as I slipped on my coat.

"Yeah...don't be out too late." She said never looking up from the book that she was reading.

"I'm not." I assured her. "What's that you're reading that has you all sucked in?"

"The name of it is Salty by an author named Aleta Williams." She looked up at me finally. Her eyes glowing with excitement! "It's a good book too, now stop bothering me so that I can finish reading and get started on the two free books that Black Expressions sent me in the mail yesterday!"

I shook my head. This woman loved to read. "That's where all of our money is going to…in books." I teased her. "You got so many dag on books that we barely have room for anything else. I'm starting to think that you have a problem."

She flipped her book over and laid it down on the sofa and then looked up at me. She looked so sexy with her hair pulled back into a ponytail, wearing one of my big shirts and a pair of footies. "I see you aren't going to hush so that I can finish reading my book. Now as far as me having a problem, it could be worse. I could be out running the streets and giving my goodies away!"

"Yeah and you could get your head knocked off! Don't play

with me girl!" I said grabbing her and tonguing her down. I laid her back on the sofa, kissing her on her chin and then her neck.

She started pushing me off of her. "Tre move! You are going to mess up my book!"

"What?"

"Move boy! My book is on the sofa and you have me lying on top of it! That will mess up the cover!"

"Lord have mercy!" I said letting her up. "The kids are gone and we have the opportunity to get it in right here on the sofa and all you can worry about is your book!" I laughed because she never ceased to amaze me.

"We can get it in later when you get home! Right now Salty is calling my name!" She picked up her book from the sofa.

"Yeah well I'm *salty* that I can't get no pussy because my wife would rather read."

She smiled at me, biting on her bottom lips. "I like the sound of that...*my wife.*"

"I bet you do. You should know something though...a real

wife would never choose a book over sexing her husband." I teased but there was some seriousness to my statement.

"I'll keep that in mind. Now toss me those chocolate chip cookies over there by the TV on your way out the door and stop whining!" I tossed her the cookies on my way out and locked the door.

On my way to Casper's house I stopped by the Red Barn, a gas station that sold food. It was right up the street from where he lived. When I pulled into the parking lot I saw Casper's cherry red 2007 Chevy Impala. I got out of my car leaving the motor running. On my way in I spoke to my boy Tyson who was posted up in front of the store.

"What's good my nig?" I asked giving him some dap. I knew without asking what he was doing. He didn't care if it was raining, sleeting, or snowing he was going to make money.

He took a pull of the Newport that he was holding. "Ain't shit. Just chillin, trying to get this money. Where you headed?"

"I'm bout to head up here to Casper's crib for a minute and

see what them niggas talkin about?"

"That's what's up. I might come through a little bit later on."
He nodded his head towards the store. "Tamika's nasty ass just
went in. That hoe ain't shit! She was eyeing me like I owed her ass
something."

I laughed. I knew the look that he was talking about all too
well because she always gave me the same look every time that I
saw her. "Man, I don't even see why Casper is even fucking with
her. He knows that she has fucked Cameron, Skeet and Rick! Her
ass be doing everything that she can to get my attention whenever
she sees me but I don't pay her ass no mind. There's just some shit
that I won't do and her ass is one of them!"

"I know that's right." He agreed. "I did hear that the hoe has
some fiyah head though. I heard that she will suck the skin off of a
dick for a lollipop!"

Just as I was about to respond, Tamika came out of the store.
"Hey Tre." She smiled as she sashayed past me, giving me the
same look that she always did. As she walked away I noticed the

extra sway in her hips. She was phat as hell, there was no denying

that. The black and white zebra print pants that she was wearing fit

her like a second layer of skin and the black top that she wore

stopped just above her belly button. Her hair was laid to perfection,

not a piece out of place. The stiletto boots that she wore clicked

against the pavement as she walked towards Casper's Impala. She

was way over dressed for somebody just making a run to the

corner store. I'd break Kisha's neck if I ever caught her in some

shit like that!

"Now she knows damned well that it's too cold out here for

that lil ass shirt that she has on!" Tyson said shaking his head.

"That shit ain't sexy at all! That bitch just looks stupid!"

He had a point, it was way too cold for the shirt that Tamika

was wearing but everybody knew what that was about...attention.

She was one of those chicks who would go to any extent to get

some attention regardless of what she had to do. "Man, you are

crazy!" I laughed. "Look, I'm going to holla at you later on when

you come through."

"Alright my man, be easy." He said still looking at Tamika as she backed out of the parking lot. He had a look of disgust on his face. I was beginning to wonder if something had gone down between the two of them. I thought about asking but then decided against it. Even if something had gone down it wasn't any of my business. We gave each other dap and then I went ahead inside the store. I knew that I was going to be drinking once I got to Casper's so I decided to get me something to eat. I ordered two hotdogs all the way and got a bag of chips. Once my food was ready I paid for my stuff and left. I smashed both hotdogs on the way up the street.

When I got to Casper's, he and the rest of the fellas were down in the basement playing Spades and getting fucked up. I sat down and joined right in. By ten that night I was so fucked up that I passed out on the sofa down in the basement.

I was awakened by the feel of soft lips around my dick. I opened my eyes but couldn't see shit because the room was dark. "Mmmm…Kisha…baby that shit feels good." I moaned resting my head on the back of the sofa. I could still feel the effects of the alcohol that I had consumed earlier. She didn't respond instead she opened her mouth wider and went all the way down on my dick until her forehead was touching the bottom of my stomach. She relaxed her throat muscles and took my dick down her throat like a pro. My toes were curled so tightly that I heard them pop! I grabbed the back of her head and tried to shove my dick even further down her throat. "Oh fuck, your mouth feels good! Damn…baby!" I held on to her hair as I fucked the back of her throat. That shit was feeling so good that I pushed her head away. I wasn't ready to come just yet. She let my dick slip from her lips. She used her spit as a lubricant as she stroked my throbbing erection. Her mouth was now on my balls licking and sucking. I wasn't sure what had gotten into her but I loved it. She'd never given me head like this before. The slurping noises that she was making were about to drive me over the edge! "Baby…I'm about to cum…put it back in your mouth." She did like I asked. She sucked on just the head while continuing to stroke me with her hand. It didn't take long for me to release my load down her throat.

"Ooooooh….shit!" I yelled as I came. She continued sucking until she had gotten every drop. I was so spent after busting that nut that I laid there and fell right back to sleep.

The next time that I woke up Casper was standing over me shaking me. "Wake yo drunk as up nigga!" Casper was a heavy dude so he was kind of heavy-handed. He slapped me on my arm. "Nigga wake up!" He laughed. "Shit ain't nobody tell yo ass to try and hang with the big dawgs!"

I sat up and looked around, wiping my eyes and trying to figure out where the hell I was at! I looked around the basement and saw empty red cups, beer cans and bottles, empty pizza boxes, and the cards still on the table. Then I looked up at Casper. That's when it hit me that I was still at Casper's house and hadn't gone home. "Fuck!" I mumbled immediately thinking about Kisha and how pissed off she was going to be. *Wait a minute.* I thought to myself. *I remember Kisha giving me some head last night. How in the fuck…*

"Y'all can come on upstairs and eat." Tamika announced

walking down the steps into the basement. She was wearing a pair of blue shorts that barely covered her ass cheeks, a wife beater and a pair of fluffy white bedroom shoes. Her legs glistened like she'd just oil them down in Johnson & Johnson baby oil. This morning her long weave was swept up in a ponytail. She flashed me a million dollar smile. "Tre, you don't need to drink! Your tail was passed out before eleven o'clock!"

Casper burst into laughter nodding his head. "Baby, I was just saying the same thing this nigga can't hang!"

I looked from Casper to Tamika as they both laughed at what he'd just said. I didn't find shit funny. I was still thinking about the events that had taken place only a few hours ago. Being that my black ass hadn't gone home and had been passed out on the sofa all night that could only mean one thing. It had been Tamika's nasty ass sucking my dick, not Kisha! I shook my head unable to believe that nasty bitch would stoop so low as to take advantage of me while I was drunk and passed out! Not only that but right in my boy's crib! This hoe was a real piece of work!

"Damn man, say something!" Casper joked. "You're still drunk ain't you?"

I looked on the sofa next to me and grabbed my hat and put it on. "Nah, I'm straight." I ran my hand over my face. I was still having a hard time trying to digest what Tamika had done. I looked up at her nasty ass and she had the nerve to wink at me. I thought about calling her sorry as out but then I thought to myself that may be a bad idea. Casper already knew the type of chick she was and he'd still decided to wife her so who's to say that if I told him what she'd done that he would believe me. Hell, he may even be ready to fight me over this bitch. I stood up and got my coat that had been draped over the back of one of the chairs. "I'm going to holla at you later man." I told Casper as I slipped on my coat. I felt my pockets for my keys and didn't feel them.

"What are you looking for?" Tamika asked.

"My keys." I took my phone out of my coat pocket to see how many messages Kisha had sent me because I knew that she'd sent several but my phone was dead. This wasn't good at all!

"They probably fell out of your pocket down in the chair." She walked over to the sofa and bent over, digging in the sofa for my keys. Her ass cheeks hanging out of her shorts. I looked at Casper as if to say, do you see this shit? He acted as if he didn't see anything wrong. "Here they go." She turned around dangling my keys.

I took my keys from her not even bothering to say thanks. Honestly I wanted to smack this nasty bitch! I looked at Casper. "I'll hit you up later homie."

"Aight man. You sure that you don't want to stay and have some breakfast? Mika cooked sausage, eggs, and grits!" He offered.

"Nah, I'm good. I know Kisha is already pissed." What I really wanted to say was, *"This nasty bitch just got finished deep-throating my sausage!"* But instead I kept my mouth closed.

"You know she is." He agreed. "But it wasn't like you could've driven home."

"Yeah but she isn't going to want to hear that shit. Well, I'm out." I gave him some dap and left.

Tre

I stuck my key in the lock and turned it slowly. I took a deep breath before pushing the door open and going inside. I wasn't sure of what I should expect. I'd left home the day before just before five o'clock in the afternoon and now here it was noon the next day. The first thing that greeted me when I walked in the house was the smell of food cooking, next came the boys. They raced to me, jumping all over me.

"Daddy! Daddy!" They both yelled.

"What's good fellas?" I asked scooping them both up in my arms. "Show your pops some love." They both gave me a big hug. I put them back down.

Shaun was digging in my coat pocket. "Where were you? Did you bring us something back?"

I playfully smacked his hand. "Boy if you don't get out of my pocket! I am going to chop your little hands off!"

"Daddy, grandma said that your black self act like you don't know how to come by or call and check on your mama no more!"

I looked at him and laughed because that sounded just like something my mama would say. "Oh for real? Well thanks for telling me. I guess that means that I am going to have to give her a call then or maybe later on we can ride over there."

They both jumped up and down. "Yay!"

"Hey daddy, guess what?" Shaun said getting excited.

"What?" I asked finally taking my coat off and tossing it on the sofa. I took a seat and the boys climbed up on my lap. I looked around noticing how nice and clean everything was. That was a dead giveaway that Kisha was mad as hell. She always cleaned when she was pissed. I tried to push that out of my head for the time being and enjoy my boys.

"Papa got a pool table and he let us play!"

"He did?"

"Yup!" Quan added. "I already know how to play too. I beat

Papa this many times." He said holding up three fingers.

"Nah-uh, no you didn't!" Shaun yelled at Quan.

"Yes I did...shut-up!"

"You shut up!" Shaun pushed Quan.

"Alright! Alright! Alright! Y'all both quit it!" I scolded them. "Y'all know better! Shaun, you keep your hands to yourself before I pop your butt!"

"But...he was telling a story! He didn't beat Papa three times! He can't even play!" Shaun was always determined to have the last word. He had a mouth like his mama but he got his temper from me.

"I did too!" Quan screamed his eyes starting to tear up.

"Shaun, what did I just say?" I asked giving him a look that told him that he was close to an ass whooping if he did be quiet.

"You said to quit." He responded just above a whisper dropping his head.

"Alright then, that's what I mean for you to do. Stop teasing your brother all of the time. How would you like it if he teased you all of the time?"

He shrugged his shoulders. "I don't know."

"Well I know. You wouldn't like it so stop doing it to him. Understand?"

He nodded his head. "Yes."

I turned my attention to Quan. "Quan what have I told you about crying every time that someone says something that you don't like?"

"You said not to." He was wiping his eyes.

"That's right! There are going to be a lot of people in life that are going to do and say things that you don't like but you can't go through life crying about it. You've got to toughen up."

Kisha came into the living room carrying a bottle of spray Lysol in one hand and a rag in the other. She had on a pair of yellow cleaning gloves, grey sweats, an old faded t-shirt, a pair of pink bedroom shoes and a scarf tied around her hair. "Oh you finally decided to bring your ass home?"

I knew it was about to be on. "Boys, y'all go in your room

and play while I talk to your mama."

"Yeah, y'all go in your room while I listen to what lies your sorry ass daddy have all lined up to tell me about where his black ass was all night!" She said with her neck and eyes rolling at the same time. If looks could kill I would've been one dead motherfucka!

Shaun giggled. "Daddy everybody calls you black!"

"Boy go in your room and close the door!" They both ran down the hall to their room and slammed the door.

Kisha stood there looking at me, I could tell that she had been crying because her eyes were red and puffy. "Baby, listen…"

"Baby…my motherfuckin' ass!" She exploded! "I am so sick and tired of this endless cycle! Shit will be all good for a while and then…" She snapped her fingers. "Just like that you go and do something to fuck it up! Every single fucking time! Yesterday when you told me that you were going over to Casper's, I didn't say a word. You'd been doing so good, spending time with me and the boys, cooking, cleaning and helping out around the house. I felt like you more than deserved some time with the fellas so I didn't complain at all. But damn I had no idea that you needed an entire night with the fellas!"

"Kisha baby, if you would just let me explain." I stood up and walked over to her. I tried to touch her arm but she snatched away!

"Don't touch me!" She rolled her eyes hard folding her arms.

I ran my hands over my head. "Listen, I got so fucked up last night that I passed out on the sofa in Caper's basement. That's where I was all night...I swear!"

She sucked her teeth and shook her head. "That is no fucking excuse Tre! You ain't some damn lil kid! You are a grown ass man! You should know your limit and know when it's time to quit! Your ass shouldn't have been passed out on Casper's sofa! You should've been at home in your bed lying next to me!" She paused and then continued. "Let me ask you a question."

I let out a frustrated breath. "Go ahead."

She looked me directly in my eyes. "How would you feel if I

stayed out all night long? No phone call, no text message, smoke signal, or nothing. All you knew is when I walked out of the house the day before I told you that I would be back in a little while. Aside from thinking that I may be out creeping, wouldn't you be worried sick? Wondering if I was okay?" She paused and looked at me. All I could do was drop my head. I hadn't even taken the time to think of it like that. "The next time that you decide that you want to stay out all night, when you do get back all that will be here waiting for your ass is this empty ass house! I'm getting tired Tre! Tired! I am a damn good woman and mother and all I ask is that you treat me how you want to be treated. That's not too much to ask for! I've been putting up with your shit for years now and just when I think that you have all of the bullshit out of your system, you go and do something else stupid!"

I couldn't argue with that because she was right. She'd put up with a lot from my ass and she really didn't deserve to be treated like this. Listening to her break it down like she did made me understand exactly why she was so upset and she had every right to be. If I'd quit drinking when I felt myself getting too drunk and brought my ass home then Tamika wouldn't have gotten the opportunity to do the nasty shit that she had. I'd definitely learned my lesson. "Baby, you're right and I apologize for causing you to worry. I promise you that it won't happen again."

"Hmph, you'd better hope not!" She said giving me nasty look and then walking back down the hallway.

I flopped back down on the sofa. "Man, fuck!" I mumbled. Even when I had every intention of doing the right thing, I still managed to fuck up! My head was killing me so I stretched out on the sofa. I reached back and got my coat and put it over my head. In no time I had drifted off to sleep.

When I woke up a few hours later, I sat up on the sofa and looked around. Wiping my eyes and stretching I looked at the window and saw that it was starting to get dark outside. I looked up at the clock on the wall and saw that it was almost seven o'clock. I'd slept all damn afternoon. I got up and went down the hall to the bathroom and took a nice hot shower. When I was done,

I got dressed in a pair of baggy grey sweats, a white tee and a pair of grey and white Adidas. I brushed my hair and put on my grey durag.

I'd heard Kisha and the boys in the boy's room when I'd come down the hallway. I went to the boy's door and slowly pushed open the door. They were on the floor along with Kisha playing Bingo.

"Hey, I ain't trying to interrupt y'all or anything but I was about to run to mama's house for a little while and I wanted to take the boys with me."

Kisha had changed clothes and was now wearing a little blue sundress. She still had her hair tied up. She looked up at me briefly. "You can take them but keep in mind that they have school in the morning and it's already passed seven."

The boys jumped up and started to put on their shoes.

"Did you want to go with us?" I asked Kisha hoping that she would say yes. I didn't like when she was upset with me because she was the type that stayed mad forever.

She started to pick the Bingo cards and chips up. "Nah, I'm going to stay here. I have a slight headache." I got down on the floor and started to help her clean up the game. "I got it."

"I know baby but I just wanted to help you."

She stopped what she was doing and looked at me. "For real, I don't even want to be around you right now. So stop trying to talk to me and just let me be. You can't do fucked up stuff and then expect for everything to be all good!" I tried to touch her again but again she snatched back. "Didn't I ask you earlier not to touch me?"

I held my hands up. "My bad...I won't touch you again."

"Good!"

I saw that me trying to talk to her was only making the situation worst so I decided to leave her alone. "Alright then, we'll see you when we get back."

"Yeah..."

I got up off the floor. "Y'all come on." I told the boys. We left and went to my mom's house. She'd cooked a big dinner so I ate there. The boys had already eaten before they left home but they still ate some of my mom's pineapple cake. She made the best pineapple cake hands down! After we'd eaten, me, my dad, and the boys played around with the pool table for a while.

My mama came into the back room where we were playing pool. "Boys, y'all come on here and get in the tub. I've already ran you some water. Quan, you go and get in grandma's tub. Shaun, you go and get in the other tub. I've already laid your night clothes in the bathroom. When y'all get out of the tub, go in your room and go to bed. I'll take y'all to school in the morning. How does that sound?"

They both started jumping up and down! "Yay!"

"Are you going to pick us up tomorrow from school too?" Quan asked. "I want to come back and play pool!"

My mama looked at my dad, placing her hand on her wide hip. "See Gerald what you done started with that pool table." She laughed. "Now we can't get rid of these two munchkins!"

"Munchkins?" The boys giggled.

"Take your little butts and get in the tub like I told you to five minutes ago!" She told the boys. They left the room going to do what she'd said.

My dad stood on the other end of the table laughing. "Those little guys are a mess."

"Yes they are." I agreed.

"Tre, tell Kisha to have the boys backpacks ready in the morning so that I can stop by and pick them up on my way to take them to school." My mama told me.

"Okay, I'll tell her."

She walked over and gave me a hug and kiss. "Well I'm glad that you came over but I am about to go and put these munchkins to bed and then go in my room and find me a good movie to watch."

"Okay." I hugged and kissed her back. "Love you."

"Love you too."

She left out and then me and my dad started to play a real game of pool, before we had just been messing around with the boys. While we were playing I told him about what was going on with me and Kisha. I even told him about what had happened with Tamika. "Man pops, I don't know what to do. I mean, I honestly went over there to have a few drinks with the fellas, enjoy myself and go home. I had no intentions on getting that messed up. It just crept up on me!"

My dad took his handkerchief out of his pocket and wiped sweat from his face before shoving it back in his pocket. I was the spitting image of my dad, same height, build, and complexion. The only difference was that he was older and had started to get grey. "I know how that can be…trust me. This Tamika girl sounds like somebody that you need to stay as far away from as you possibly can. She sounds like trouble. I don't know any woman who would go that far to mess with a man to wait til he's drunk and passed out and take advantage of him." He shook his head. "Stay away from her!"

"You ain't got to tell me. That's exactly what I plan to do!"

"You know, when you try to do right there is always going to be something that tries and prevent you from doing that. Now I have to tell you. You have been doing good. I have noticed that you have been spending more time with your family and I am very proud of you son. I know that you are young but trust me, there ain't nothing out there in them streets but trouble. You have a good woman at home, don't mess that up. I know that we all make mistakes and that's life. If you didn't make mistakes then that would mean that you ain't human! Don't let what just happened discourage you. Keep doing like you've been doing. Kisha won't stay mad forever. It will all blow over soon but stay away from this Tamika because something ain't right about her!"

We continued to talk while we finished up our game of pool. I didn't leave until a little after eleven. As I drove home I thought about all of the things that my pops had told me. He was right I had been doing too good to let what had happened the night before discourage me. I decided that I'd just give Kisha sometime to cool off but in the meantime I'd continue to do like I'd been doing.

Lala

Two weeks had gone by since me finding out that I was pregnant with twins. One baby was okay, I felt like I could handle that but two! I'd been devastated since Dr. Porter delivered the news. I kept wondering how in the hell I was going to take care of two babies, plus work. Nisey had been trying to comfort me as much as she possibly could. She even offered to help me with the babies as far as babysitting. I appreciated her offer but the truth of the matter was, she was about to have a baby of her own to take care of. There was no way she would be able to care for three babies by herself while I worked. That would be too much on her and there was no way that I could ask her to do that. I'd just have to figure out something by the time the babies got here.

It was Tuesday evening and Nisey had been kind enough to

invite me over to her place for dinner. When I arrived she greeted

me at the door wearing a white tee, blue sweats, bedroom shoes

and a red and white cooking apron with *Nisey* stitched across the

front. "Hey girl." She smiled holding open the door for me.

"Hey. I like that apron." I replied walking inside.

"Thanks."

Her home was really nice and cozy. It wasn't anything fancy

but it was nicely decorated and really neat. The eggshell paint on

the walls gave it a warm relaxed vibe. The first thing that I noticed

when I walked into her living room was the huge bookshelf that

took up one entire wall.

"Goodness you sure love to read, don't you?" I asked

walking over to the bookshelf and looking at all of the different

books. She had a wide variety.

"Girl, I will read anything, Sci-Fi, romance, drama, mystery,

erotica, street-lit. Honey, it doesn't matter! I just love to read!" She

stood rubbing her belly. "Go on and take off your coat and make

yourself at home. The food's done so we can go on and ea if you want."

I took off my coat and laid it down on the back of the sofa. I walked around looking at the pictures on the wall. There were lots of pictures of her, her son and her husband. I was surprised to see that her husband was white. He was tall with red hair and freckles. He looked kind of nerdy to me but you can't judge a book by its cover. "You had a beautiful family. Y'all looked so happy." I said staring at the photos.

"Thanks." She stood there staring at the pictures for a moment, a look in her eyes like she was reminiscing but then she snapped out of it. "Come on let's go into the kitchen."

"Alright." I followed her down the short hallway into the kitchen. The kitchen was decorated with an apple theme. There were apples everywhere. It was really cute but not something I would've chosen. The table had already been set so I took a seat.

"I hope you're hungry because I fixed baked chicken, peas and carrots, mashed potatoes, rolls, cherry cobbler and to drink we're having Juicy Juice." She laughed.

I laughed too. "That sounds great. I appreciate you inviting me to dinner. I haven't had a good home cooked meal since I left Nita's house. Most of the time I eat fast food…well all of the time."

"That isn't healthy for you or those babies. They need some good ol' home cooking!" She fixed both of our plates and then sat down at the table. We said grace and then started to eat.

"Yeah, I know it isn't healthy. I will be so glad when I get back on my feet." I put a forkful of peas and carrots in my mouth. I took my time chewing as I thought about how messed up my life seem to be at the moment. I shook my head. "Sometimes I can't tell if I am coming or going but I'll tell you one thing. I have definitely learned a lot from this entire experience."

Nisey chewed her food before responding. "Well that's what life is all about, living and learning." She took a sip of her juice. "Why don't you tell me exactly how you ended up here? I mean you've told me bits and pieces but tell me everything. That way you can stop carrying everything around on the inside because that isn't good. We all need someone that we can talk to without feeling like we are being judged and in your case that's me. I have made my fair share of mistakes and so I am in no position to judge anyone. As a matter of fact I will share my story with you when you are done. How does that sound?"

"Sounds great." I took a deep breath and then I began. I told her everything from the first day that Tre and I met up until the last time that I saw him. When I was done I had tears streaming down my face. I don't think I really realized up until that point how much I really missed him. "I know that it was messed up for me to be dealing with another woman's man and then on top of falling in love with him I ended up pregnant but I never meant for it to go down this way. I mean, I never planned to fall for him or get pregnant. The plan was to just have a little fun and that's it. I didn't have anybody and he was there and to be honest I was very attracted to him. I won't sit here and front like I didn't want to have sex with him because I did but I tried to fight it! I really did! Even when he first approached me I said no because you have somebody but I just couldn't keep saying no." Nisey had been quiet the entire time, never saying a word just listening. "I know that you probably think I am some kind of home wrecking hoe, don't you?"

"Actually, I don't. I mean, I'm not going to sit here and say that you weren't wrong for getting involved with this man knowing that he had someone but ultimately the decision was his. He was the one who was in a committed relationship, not you. At the end of the day if he didn't care about the woman that he had at home, why should you? That may sound harsh but it is what it is."

Finally someone who saw shit the way that I saw it! "True and that's how I felt about the situation. Honestly, I don't feel like I owe her anything but on the flipside of that there is a part of me that is like what if I was in her shoes. How would I feel about the next bitch creeping with my man and getting pregnant by him? I know without a doubt that I would be hurt but I would never go and approach her or anything because I know better than that, I would fuck my man up though!"

"Yeah, I hate when women be fighting each other over a dude but still be laid up with him like he ain't did shit wrong! That burns me up!" She hit her fist on the table. "I have to commend you for how you handled things. A lot of women would've been at his door telling the babymama that she was pregnant and just causing a huge messy scene. I like the fact that you didn't do that."

"Nah, that ain't how I roll. You see one thing about it. I've always known my position from day one. I knew that I was the side chic, the one that he crept off with, do what he do and then go back home to ol girl. I've always played my position and never tried to play any other position. Most chics be a side chic with main chic expectations…not me! When I realized that I'd fallen in love with Tre and was pregnant by him. I packed my shit and dipped because I knew that it wouldn't be long before I did some ol silly shit that I would regret later! I'd been known that I was in love with him a while back, hell we been dealing for two years but then when I found out I was pregnant…I just had to leave. I will be honest with you though, I miss him a lot. I miss laughing and talking to him."

"That's understandable. So do you plan on telling him that you're pregnant?"

"No...I don't know...maybe one day."

She sat back in her chair. "What about your parents? From the things that you've told me about them, they seem like they'd be really supportive and you need all of the support that you can get during this time. Plus I know that your mom is going to be very upset that her only daughter, her only child, kept her first pregnancy from her. This is a very special time in your life and hers. These are her first grandbabies. I think that you should tell your parents."

I sat there thinking about what she'd just suggested and even though I knew that my parents would be very supportive. I also knew that my mom would be trying to get me to come back home. She wouldn't be feeling the idea of me being three and a half hours away in Danville, VA, living in a motel room, pregnant! Oh no, she would have a damn fit sure as hell and I wasn't trying to go through all of that with her. "I don't know. My mom will hit the roof when I tell her and especially knowing how my living conditions are here."

"Lala, you need to tell your parents. You are twenty-eight years old, it's not like they are going to beat you or anything." Nisey joked but I knew that she meant what she was saying. "Listen you are grown and so ultimately the decision is yours but I think that you should consider telling your parents. Let them help you. That's what they are there for. I can see that you are a strong independent woman who feels like she can handle everything on her own. You feel like you made this mess and so it is up to you to clean it up but there is nothing wrong with having a helping hand."

"You're right." I agreed. "I'm going to call my mom sometime this week and talk to her. I just have to build up my nerve first." I laughed nervously. "So tell me your story."

I noticed her entire demeanor change and a sad expression covered her face. "Well my story is very similar to yours. I met my husband Jonathan six and a half years ago when I was working at

Starbucks. He would come in all the time and we would talk,
nothing really serious just general conversation. Eventually I began
looking forward to him coming in. We became really close and
found out that we had a lot in common. At the time he was married
to his ex-wife Sylvia. He'd told me about her and the problems that
they were having. He'd said that the marriage had been dead for
years and that it no longer felt like a marriage but more less like
they were roommates. I would give him advice, telling him things
that I thought might help. He told to me that he didn't even feel
like trying anymore. We were friends for a while and it was very
innocent but after a while I realized that I'd started to develop
feelings for him." She paused, took a sip of her juice and then
continued. "When I realized that I'd developed feelings for him, I
started to back off. I began avoiding his phone calls and text
messages and wouldn't see him. I even changed my shift to avoid
seeing him. Needless to say, none of it worked because one night
when I got off from work he was waiting for me in the parking lot.
He asked me what was going on and why I'd been avoiding him.

Instead of lying, I told him the truth. To my surprise he confessed that he'd also developed feelings for me. That night was the start of a seven month affair. I wasn't satisfied with being the woman on the side that he came and got his rocks off with and then went back home to his wife. I wanted to be number one! So I gave him an ultimatum, I told him that it was either me or his wife. The next thing I knew he was standing at my door with all of his things. A few months later I found out that I was pregnant with JJ. Jonathan filed for a divorce from Sylvia and we got engaged. No sooner than his divorce was final we got married, had a little private ceremony in his parents backyard. His parents despised me and still do to this day but they tolerate me. They've always felt like I was the reason that his marriage to Sylvia didn't work out but I strongly disagree. That shit was over before I came into the picture and they would've eventually divorced anyways! Hell, Sylvia didn't seem the least bit heartbroken by the divorce! As a matter of fact she remarried as well to some young Italian guy that she met while on vacation. She says she met him on vacation but I think her ass had been knowing him and screwing him on the low!"

I interrupted. "Did Jonathan have any kids with her?"

She shook her head. "Nah."

"Oh okay."

She continued. "Anyways, everything was great or so I thought. About ten months ago I noticed that Jonathan had started becoming very chummy with one of his co-workers. He worked at the Toyota dealership over on Piedmont Dr. Him and this little skinny white chic name Elizabeth were going out for lunch together, texting and calling each other after work. When I told him that I wasn't feeling how close the two of them had become, he told me that I was over-reacting and that the two of them were just friends. I told him that I didn't give a damn how good of friends they were she didn't need to be calling and texting him. For months we argued about this friendship that I felt like had to be something more because of how determined he was to continue the phone calls and texting, let's not forget the lunch dates. I felt like he was totally disregarding my feelings. He swore it wasn't like that. He claimed that the reason why he continued doing what I had asked him not to do was because I was acting as if I didn't trust him." She paused and looked away. I couldn't quite tell what she was looking at. She looked to have a blank stare in her eyes. Then I saw the tears in them. "Needless to say our happy marriage wasn't so happy anymore. We were constantly arguing over Elizabeth." Tears rolled freely down her cheeks. "I remember one day when we were over at mama's house and she noticed the tension between us. She asked me if everything was okay and I explained to her what was going on. I asked her if I wrong for wanting him to end the friendship with Elizabeth. She said to me, 'No baby, you were wrong for how you got this man and that is why his friendship with this woman is driving you crazy. You are afraid that he will do to you what he did to his first wife with you.'" She shook her head and wiped the tears that were on her face but it didn't do any good because they were immediately replaced by more. I too was crying by now. "I remember telling her that she was wrong and that wasn't the reason that I wanted him to end the friendship but deep down inside I knew that she was right. She'd hit the nail directly on the head! Don't get me wrong I knew that Jonathan loved me but hell he had loved Sylvia once before too!"

I interrupted, using the back of my hand to wipe my tears. "I have a quick question."

"What is it?" She asked taking another sip of her juice and rubbing her belly.

"Throughout the entire relationship had Jonathan ever given you any reason to not trust him? I mean before this Elizabeth situation came about was there anything else?"

She shook her head. "Nope…nope…not none at all. He was the perfect husband." She ran her finger through her braids and dropped her head. "That's what makes this shit even worse. I swear karma is a bitch!"

I was confused. "Huh? Nisey what do you mean?"

She lifted her head and looked over at me, tears steadily streaming down her cheeks. "The morning of the accident,

Jonathan was driving me to work and the taking JJ to school. It was raining so hard that we could barely see. He and I were arguing over a text message that Elizabeth had sent him just before we'd left home. It wasn't anything serious, it was a joke that someone had sent her and she had forwarded it to him. It didn't matter to me what it was, all that mattered to me was that she had texted him after I had plainly told him that I wanted it to stop! He kept asking me to let it go so that he could concentrate on the road but I wouldn't…" She broke down and sobbed loudly. "I wouldn't let it go! I was so mad at him…"

I got up from my seat and rubbed her back. "It's okay Nisey. Listen maybe we shouldn't talk about this anymore. Let's talk about something else."

"No, I'm fine." She cried. "I'm…fine. I want to tell you."

My heart went out to her. I didn't need to hear the rest to know that she blamed herself for the accident and the deaths of her husband and son. That had to be a hard thing to carry around on your conscience. "Okay well you can tell me later."

She shook her head. "I'm good…I'm going to tell you now." She got up and got a paper towel from the paper towel holder and wiped her face.

"Nisey where is your bathroom?"

"Right down the hall, it's the first door on your left."

I went down to the bathroom to empty my bladder while she got herself together. When I came back out of the bathroom she was sitting at the table, eyes puffy but dry. "Are you okay?" I asked.

"Yeah." She gave me a forced smile. I took my seat. "Okay, now as I was saying. We were on our way to drop me off at work and we were arguing like hell. I remember telling him that I was at the end of my rope and that if he didn't stop that bitch texting him then I was taking JJ and leaving. He took his eyes off of the briefly to look at me. He was about to say something but before he could an eighteen wheeler crashed into the side of our minivan. It hit on the driver's side, JJ was sitting behind Jonathan. I looked back just as the eighteen-wheeler crashed into us and saw the look of terror in my baby's eyes. That was the last thing I saw before I was knocked unconscious. I woke up hours later to find out that my son and husband hadn't made it."

I sat there with my hands covering my mouth, tears streaming down my cheeks again. I didn't know how to respond to what she had just told me but somehow the words, 'I'm so sorry', managed to slip from my lips.

"Yeah me too." Nisey said staring off again. "I am grateful though that God allowed this baby and I to survive through all of that. I came out of the accident with only a few scratches and bruises. The biggest scar I received was the one on my heart because no matter how much time passes it doesn't seem to heal at all." She looked at me and I could see the pain in her eyes. "Lala, there are nights where I lay down and I dream about the accident. I see everything just as it happened but at the end of my dream, I always see JJ and he's asking me why."

"Nisey, I really don't know what I can say that will make you feel better but I am here for you anytime that you need me, day or night just call and I'm here."

"Thanks girl. I appreciate that."

"No problem."

We sat at her table and continued to talk for hours. Time flew and before we knew it, it was after two in the morning. Nisey insisted that I stay with her instead of driving back to the hotel. I accepted her offer and crashed on her sofa for the night.

Lala

For the next month and a half I threw myself into working on my book. Nisey was a huge help by reading each chapter as I wrote them. She would give me her ideas and help me catch the errors that I'd made. With the story being loosely based on my relationship with Tre it made me miss him a lot as I wrote and thought about all of the times that we'd shared and memories that we'd made together. A few times I started to pick up the phone and call him but I knew that I was doing the right thing by staying away from him.

It was Saturday night and I had just finished the final chapter of my book. Nisey was sitting on the sofa reading over it. I sat across from her on the loveseat waiting to hear what she thought. The anticipation was killing me! "Hurry up Nisey!"

"Girl, be quiet! I'm reading as fast as I can!" She said

without looking up from her laptop.

I needed to do something to take my mind off of the book so I decided to call my mom while I waited for Nisey to finish. I took out my cell and dialed my mom. I got up from where I was sitting and walked into the kitchen. The phone rang several times before my mom picked up.

"Hey baby, I was just lying here thinking about you. How are you doing?" She asked sounding happy to hear from me.

"I am doing great!" I replied excitedly. "Guess what?"

"What? I am too old to be doing a lot of guessing so just tell me!" She laughed. "What are you all excited about?"

"Come on ma...guess!" I whined. I didn't want to just tell her my good news. That would take all of the fun out of it. I'd told her and my dad about the book that I was working on a few weeks earlier and they'd been thrilled about me writing a book.

"Okay, ummm...you found another job?"

"Nope."

"Met a rich man?"

I giggled into the phone. "I wish!"

"Met a handsome man with a good job and even better credit?"

"Shoot…I wish but nope!"

"Okay, give me a hint or just tell me already!"

"I finished my book!" I blurted.

"Awww…Lala that's great!" She sounded just as excited as me.

I heard my dad in the background asking. "What's great?"

"Lala finished her book!" My mom replied.

"That's my girl! Tell her that I want an autographed copy and don't forget about us little people when she becomes a famous author!"

I laughed. "Tell him he will most definitely be getting an autographed copy! Also tell him he doesn't have to worry about me forgetting anybody because no one will probably even buy this book so there is no way that I will become famous!"

"Oh hush your mouth girl talking that nonsense!" My mom's

voice took on a serious tone. "Don't speak negative about your project! Speak positive and positive things will happen! Every little thing started out small and became something bigger! Don't you dare doubt what you can become. You can become anything that you put your mind to and that includes a New York Times Best-selling Author!"

Hearing her say that made me feel empowered like I really could become a best-selling author if I wanted to. I'd done research about self-publishing my book. I'd found out how to upload my book to Kindle and Nook so that is where I planned to start. Nisey had made me a hot cover using her photoshop program so I was all set. "Thanks ma! I really appreciate that."

"You are welcomed baby. I am so proud of you! My baby is an author!" She beamed!

I couldn't help but laugh at her. "Ma, you are a mess but I must admit, I am very proud of myself. Just a couple of months ago it felt like my world was falling apart because of the bad choices that I'd made but now it feels like I am finally headed in the right direction."

"That's good baby. I am glad to see that you are not letting your mistakes hold you back from moving forward. We all make mistakes and that's alright because that is what life is all about, making mistakes and learning from them. You have taken something negative and made it into something positive and I couldn't be more proud of you for that."

I knew that it was time for me to come clean with her about my pregnancy. It was better to go ahead and get it over with. I'd hid it long enough. I took a deep breath. "Ma, I'm pregnant." I held my breath and waited for her response.

"Huh? What did you say LaQuela?"

Hearing her say my real name told me that she'd heard what I'd said but wanted to be sure that she'd heard me correctly. So I repeated myself. "I said that I'm pregnant. That's why I left Boykins."

"Oh my goodness, Lala." I heard her let out a sigh. "So you've known all this time and you are just now telling me? When did you start keeping secrets from me and your daddy? We raised you better than that!" Just that quickly the excitement about my book and how well I was doing was replaced by disappointment.

"Yes ma'am. I knew before I left but I was too ashamed and afraid to say anything…"

"Ashamed of what?" She cut me off. "Girl, I am your mama! If you can't come to me and talk to me then who in the hell can you go to? I have always been here for you! Whether you were right or wrong! I have had your back through everything! Me and your daddy have always made it clear that there was nothing so bad that you couldn't come to us! We may be disappointed in some of your choices but we are going to love you regardless! You know that!"

"Yes ma'am, I do." The waterworks had started and I now had tears meeting beneath my chin. "I apologize, ma." I sniffled.

"Oh hush that darn crying! You should've been crying when you were lying to me for months!" I heard my dad ask what was going on. "She's pregnant and we are just now finding out!"

"Pregnant? Since when and by who?" I heard him yell.

I rolled my eyes up in the ceiling. "Lord, I knew that I shouldn't have said shit." I mumbled as I listened to the two of them fuss back and forth about me hiding my pregnancy.

"Lala, what in the hell is your problem?" My dad's voice boomed through the phone. "I knew there was something else to you leaving other than what you were telling us! Did that boy put you up to this?"

"No! He doesn't even know!" I quickly defended Tre. "I didn't tell anyone. I wasn't sure if I was going to keep it or not at the time but then after I left I decided that I would."

"Okay, so how far along are you spose to be?" He asked sounding as if he was speaking through clenched teeth.

"I'm five months and one week."

"Oh my goodness girl, I don't know what to say. I can't believe that you would keep something like this from me and your mama. This is our first grandchild. Don't you think that we have the right to know?"

I wiped the tears that stained my cheeks. "I wanted to tell y'all but there was so much going on. I'd already seen the disappointed looks on your faces when I'd told you about Tre and me. I just didn't want to see those looks again. I'm sorry daddy. I really am." I cried.

He let out a frustrated breath. "Oh hush up that crying now. It's going to be alright but don't you be hiding things like this from us. Your mama is over here upset and crying. It's one thing to have you up there living in a hotel but on top of that you're pregnant. That's not good."

"I know." I wiped my face again.

"Now I know that you have been saying that you didn't want any help from me and your mama but it's not up to you anymore. I refuse to have you living in a hotel pregnant with my grandbaby. We are going to help you get a place and the things that you need for this baby, okay."

"Okay." There was no way that I was going to argue with him right now. I also decided to leave out the fact that I was pregnant with twins. I'd tell them that part later. "Thanks daddy."

"You don't have to thank me baby. I'm doing what I am sposed to do." He explained. "Speaking of doing what I am sposed to do. Don't you think that you need to tell this boy that you are pregnant so that he can do what he's sposed to do?"

I'd known that this question was coming and I knew that he was about to get upset all over again by my answer. "Daddy, I'm not going to tell him. I can't because he has a family already and that would just mess up his home. I couldn't do that."

"That's bullshit!" He fumed. "I don't give a damn about him already having a family! This baby is his family too! He should've thought about his family at home before he went out in the streets and made another baby!"

"I know that's right!" I heard my mom cosign from the background. "If he's man enough to play, he'd better be man enough to pay!"

"You damn right he'd better!" My dad continued. "This child deserves to have a mother and a father! You owe it to your child to tell this man the truth and let him decide whether or not he wants

to be there. You have no right to take it upon yourself to decide

that. He has a right to know."

"I can't daddy."

"Lala, you are twenty-eight years old, about to bring a child

into this world. When are you going to grow up and act your age?

Grown women handle their business not run and hide like little

children! You were woman enough to lay with this man and get

pregnant, now be woman enough to do what's right. This isn't

about you anymore. It's about your child. Let that man worry

about his home and what happens after his ol' lady finds out about

this child. Hell you weren't worried about her at first! What are

you going to do hide this child forever? Does that even make

sense? What are you going to say when this child asks for its

daddy? Are you going to say I couldn't tell him about you because

he already has another family? Think about what you are going to

be doing to this child Lala."

The things that he was saying really made sense. I hadn't

thought about it that way but now he had me thinking. Maybe I should contact Tre and let him know about the babies. That way I could say that I did my part by letting him know about his children. Whether he chose to be a part of their lives would solely be up to him.

"I will give it some thought."

"Alright, you do that. I am going to talk to your mama and we will call you back tomorrow and talk some more about getting you a place."

"Alright, thanks again."

"You're welcome…I love you, Lala."

"I love you too. Tell ma, I love her too."

"I will. Good night."

"Good night." We hung up. "Thank you lord, I finally got that off of my chest. Now all I have to do is tell them that its twins. I still have a ways to go but at least now I'll have some help."

I walked back into the living room where Nisey was sitting on the sofa watching TV. When she saw me walk into the room she switched off the TV. "Chic that book is off the damn chain! I love the ending! Oh we have to upload this to Kindle and Nook tonight!"

"Girl, we can do that tomorrow. I am really not in the mood tonight. These babies are moving around like crazy and my mom and dad are mad at me…"

"Mad? Why?" Nisey asked a concerned look taking over her chubby face.

"I told them that I was pregnant."

"Sooo…why are they mad?" she looked at me waiting for an answer.

"They're mad because I kept it from them."

She started laughing and waved me off. "Girl, I thought you were talking about something. They aren't really mad. Their just a little disappointed but everything will be just fine." She sat down at the computer. "So when are they coming up here?" she asked as she powered up the laptop.

"Huh?" I asked confused. I stood behind her with one hand

on her chair. "What are you talking about?"

She turned to look at me briefly before turning her attention back to the computer screen. "Girl, you know just like I do that your mama will be up here with the quickness now that she knows you're pregnant!"

"Oh, I have no idea when they are coming but my dad said that they are going to help me get a place."

"That's good." She went to the Kindle website. "Okay now create your account."

She got up and I sat down. I put in all of the information that they asked for and uploaded my book cover and files. Then I hit save and publish. When I was done I turned and looked at Nisey. "Well it's done!" I said excitedly!

"Almost, now go to Pubit.com so that you can upload to Nook as well! Girl we about to let everybody know who Lala Chambers is! Okaaay!" She raised her hand for a high five. I smacked her hand and then turned back around to the computer. When I was done at Pubit.com, Nisey and I both looked at each other and started screaming! "Awwww snap! My girl is an author! We can go through the paperback process tomorrow so that you can order copies and we can go out and sell them to people. Pretty soon you can say good bye to your job at the hotel!" She sounded more excited than I was.

"I sure hope so but how are people going to find out about the book?" I asked.

"Facebook, Twitter and word-of-mouth! We about to do the damn thing!" She squealed. "I am so proud of you and happy to be the friend of a soon to be famous author!"

All I could do was blush.

Part 2

BabyMama Drama

Lala

Two Months Later...

Things were finally starting to look up for me. My mom and dad had helped me get a nice two story house with three bedrooms, one and a half baths, a den, living room, kitchen, basement and one car garage. The rent was a little steep but they were paying half every month. The best thing that had happened was my book was doing great! It was selling like hotcakes, getting mostly five star reviews. I couldn't believe the amount when I looked at my royalties for the first month. All I could do was thank God because for a first time author that no one knew, I was doing the damn thing! With the first book doing so well I'd decided to do a part two. In a lot of the reviews people were asking about a part two. I figured that it only made sense to give the people what they wanted and make this money while it lasted.

Nisey was still hanging in there right by my side, doing everything that she could to help me and make my book a success. I couldn't begin to describe how much I appreciated her. She'd turned out to be a true blessing.

Two weeks ago, she'd given birth to a 7lb. 8oz little boy. She named him Evan. Of course I was right by her side through it all, her mom and brother came to the hospital but I was surprised to see that none of Jonathan's family showed up. I called his parents like Nisey asked me to but no one answered each time that I called and I left several voicemails. Still no one called back. I started to wonder would things be that way after I told Tre about my pregnancy. I wondered if he would want nothing to do with my babies or how his family would react once they found out. It scared me just thinking about how ugly things could get. I didn't want to deal with any drama at all but I knew that I had to come clean about my pregnancy. A lot of the things that my parents had told me concerning the reasons why he should know made a lot of sense. I did owe it to my children. I'd planned to take a trip back home this weekend to talk to him.

I moved around my room preparing to hit the road for my long drive home back to Boykins. My Bluetooth was in my ear so that I could talk to Nisey while I packed my last minute things.

"Did you already put the books in the car?" Nisey asked. "You know that everybody and their mama are going to be bugging you for a copy! Everybody is going to be treating you like a celebrity when you get back home!"

"Yeah I put the books in the car last night." I responded dryly not really too excited about going back home to face Tre. I wanted to see everybody back home because I did miss my family but knowing what had to be done and not knowing how he would respond was making me dread going.

"Why do you sound so down?" Nisey asked. I heard Evan start to cry. "Awww don't cry mama's little man." I waited until she got him quiet.

"Is little man alright?" I asked. I'd fallen in love with her baby and couldn't wait to meet my own. I'd found out at my last visit that both babies were girls. I was overly excited about having two little girls to spoil and shop for.

"Yeah he's fine. He's wet, that's all." She replied. "Now tell me, what's the matter with you? Is this about Tre?"

I sat down on my bed beside my small bag that I was packing. "Yes, girl I am so nervous. I have no idea how he is going to respond once I tell him about these babies. I mean I'm not just pregnant but pregnant with twins! Not only that but he may think that these babies aren't even his being that I left!" I shook my head. "I don't know Nisey."

"Don't know what? Look, go down and there talk to him. If he doesn't believe you then tell him you will holla at him once those babies are born and he can have a blood test done…simple as that!"

"All of that sounds good but you and I both know that shit is never that simple." I reminded her. "I can already feel that this shit isn't going to go well. I have a feeling that he is going to be on some bullshit! I have been trying to do the right thing and keep the drama to a minimum but if he gets stupid I don't know how I am going to react!"

I heard her let out a frustrated breath. "Lala, I ain't trying to be mean or anything but grow up! Stop sitting around whining and trying to predict what will happen and handle your business! You have been running from this situation long enough. Now it's time to step up to the plate. You knew when you decided to keep these babies that you would eventually have to tell this man about them, so do it!"

I felt slightly offended by her words but how could I argue with her when I knew that what she was saying was right. I'd made my bed and now it was time to lie in it. "I'm not whining." I corrected her. "I just have a not so good feeling about this trip that's all." I let out a sigh. "Look, I'll holla at you later. I need to finish getting my things together and get on the road."

"Alright, call me whenever you stop to let me know that you

are okay. I will be praying for you to have a safe trip."

"Thanks."

"No problem. You're my girl and I love you."

"I love you too." We hung up and I finished packing my things. I put everything in the car, checked the house to make sure that I had unplugged everything and then I headed out the door.

Tre

Things between Kisha and I were finally back on track. The only problem was she had gotten a new best friend...Tamika. I'm not sure how this shit happened! One day I came home and heard giggling coming from the kitchen, at first I'd thought that it was Kisha and the boys but then I heard another female voice that sounded kind of familiar. I stuck my head in the kitchen and saw Tamika braiding Kisha's hair. They were laughing and giggling like they'd been best friends for years. Tamika looked at me with a slick ass smirk on her face.

"Hey Tre."

"What's up?" I spoke but not really wanting to. What I really wanted to do was ask this nasty bitch to leave! Seeing her made me think back to the night that I'd gotten drunk and passed out on

Casper's sofa.

"Bae, you know I've wanted to get my hair braided for a while now. I am so glad that I ran into Tamika today at Food Lion." Kisha explained. "Tamika and I go way back. We used to be good friends back in middle school but once we got to high school we started to run in different circles."

"Hmph." I responded thinking to myself it's good that she decided to run in a different circle or she probably would've turned out to be a hoe just like Tamika!

"Is everything alright baby?" Kisha asked. I assume that the expression on my face reflexed how I was feeling on the inside because I definitely was not feeling Tamika being up in my house.

"Yeah everything is straight." I lied and left the two of them in the kitchen.

From that day about a month ago until now, every time I look Tamika is sitting her funky ass up in my house. She hasn't tried anything or said anything out of the way but I still don't trust her. I know that bitch is up to no good. She can smile up in Kisha's face all she wants with her fake ass but the first time that she steps out

of line I am putting her dirty ass in her place like I should've a

long time ago!

It was Friday afternoon and I was laid back on the sofa

chillin watching TV because I didn't have to go in to work. Kisha

was sitting on the other end of the sofa with her feet in my lap

reading a book when the doorbell rang. Kisha looked up from her

book. "Baby can you get that? I don't feel like getting up. I finally

got my copy of Confessions of A Side Chic today! I am just

getting to the good part, LeLe is finally about to tell Trent that

she's pregnant by him! Ooooooh…I hope his girlfriend Karma

whoop LeLe's ass when she finds out!" She went on and on about

the book she was reading. Sometimes I believe that Kisha thought

the shit that she read in those books were real because she would

be so damn hyped about it!

I shook my head as I got up, placing Kisha's feet on the sofa.

"You seriously need some counseling woman." I laughed at my

baby, who damn near had her whole face in the book! She waved me off. The doorbell rang again. I walked to the door and peeped out of the peep hole. I saw Tamika standing on the other side of the door. "Gotdamn this bitch don't ever stay at home!" I mumbled as I unlocked the door and opened it. I didn't bother to try and hide the irritated look on my face.

"Hey Tre." Tamika smiled her eyes roaming over my bare chest. I'd taken my shirt off because Kisha had the heat turned up and it was hot inside the house. She was wearing a red halter jumper that was so tight it looked like it would split if she made any sudden moves! "Is Kisha home?"

"Yeah." I replied dryly. I stepped back out of the way and let her in. "She's lying on the sofa."

She walked past me and into the living room switching her ass as hard as she could. "Hey girl!" She squealed to Kisha.

I closed the door and followed her into the living room. I grabbed my shirt off the back of the sofa and put it on. Kisha laid her book down on the coffee table. "Hey Mika, girl that jumper is cute. Where'd you get it?"

"Chile, I've had this thing for a while. It's old." She said looking down at her outfit.

"Old or not I still like it."

"Well thanks girl. Chile, I swear you always have your head stuck in a dag on book! What's the name of that one right there?" Tamika asked pointing to the book lying on the table.

"It's called Confessions of A Side Chic by this girl named La…"

I interrupted her to let her know that I was about to go. I didn't want to be anywhere near Tamika so I always made it a point to leave whenever she was around. "Baby, I'm about to roll out for a lil while." I told Kisha as I grabbed my hat and put it on. "I'll be back in a few hours."

"Alright baby." Kisha replied. "Don't stay gone too long, I'll miss you too much!" I gave her a quick peck on the lips and was out the door.

I hadn't been going over to Casper's crib as much since the shit that had gone down with Tamika but since she was over at my spot I decided that I would go and holla at him for a minute. When I pulled up in the driveway as usual the yard was full with vehicles. His crib was where all of the fellas hung at. I parked and got out of my car and walked up on the porch. I rang the bell a few times before my homeboy Skeet opened the door.

"What's up man? Come on in." He greeted me, leaving the door open for me to come in.

"Hey." I went inside closing the door behind me. I followed him down to the basement. When I got down there everybody was doing the usual, drinking, smoking, gambling, playing the X-box and talking shit. I greeted everybody and joined right in. I'd been there for about an hour when my phone started to vibrate. I checked it and was shocked to see that it was a message from Lala.

Lala: Hey Tre, I'm sorry to bother you but I am in town and I need to see you. It's important.

For some reason her message immediately caused me to become upset. I mean she'd been gone for six and a half months and now she was back and thought that I was supposed to want to see her! Nah, she had the game fucked up! Shit had changed since she'd been gone! Kisha and I were finally doing good and I planned to keep it that way. I texted her back.

Tre: Don't text my phone anymore.

A few seconds later she texted back, **Lala: I really need to talk to you. I only need like ten minutes and then if you don't want me to bother you anymore after that I won't.**

What in the fuck was so important? What could she possibly have to say to me after all of these months of me not hearing from her? **Tre: Whatever it is I advise you text it to me now because I'm not meeting you anywhere. Honestly I don't have shit to say to you and I don't see what you could possibly have to say to me! What we had is over and done so if it's anything like that then you may as well save it!**

Lala: For real? Since when did you become such an asshole! Nigga the last thing on my mind is meeting up with you to fuck so please get over yourself! What I need to talk to you about is something way more serious than fucking! Smh!

Tre: When did I become an asshole? Lmao around the same time you decided to run off without telling a motherfucker shit! I don't know what the fuck you think this is but you can't just roll into town and expect me to come running because you text! Shit has changed! Now I am going to ask you again to stop texting my phone. Have a nice life!

Lala: FUCK YOU TRE! I GUESS THIS IS WHAT HAPPENS WHEN YOU CHOOSE TO LAY DOWN WITH KIDS!

Tre: Oh now I'm a kid but you are a grown ass woman who jumped up and moved out of town, leaving your home and your job because you claimed that you couldn't handle your feelings for this kid! Bitch please! Get a life and leave me the fuck alone!

I was about to slip my phone back in my pocket when it started to ring. Cuddy Buddy by Trey Songz played letting me know that it was Lala. I looked at the screen and contemplated whether or not to answer it. I pressed ignore and put my phone in my pocket.

"Damn nigga you done got all quiet, over there texting like some love sick teenager!" Casper teased laughing. "Let that woman breath man!"

"Nigga shut up!" I forced a laughed because my mind was far from what he was talking about. Lala's messages had me heated! My phone vibrated again, I let out a frustrated breath before reaching into my pocket to retrieve it. "Why the fuck won't she chill?" I huffed aloud.

"Oh damn…babymama trippin?" Skeet inquired.

"Nah man, this chic that I used to fuck wit blowing my damn phone up! She's about to make me cuss her ass out!" I replied checking my phone. I saw that Lala had left a voicemail. I got up and went outside to check it and to check her ass after I listened to whatever bullshit that she'd left on my voicemail. I dialed my voicemail and entered my passcode. *"I can't believe that you are playing me like this. I didn't message you to start an argument with you or cause you any trouble. You should know me better than that because for as long as you have been dealing with me, I've never brought any drama your way. I really need to speak to you about something very important but I guess…"* Her voice cracked and I could hear her sniffling. *"You know what, never mind. I guess this is the way that you treat bitches…it's funny how I am a bitch now but never once in the two years that we were dealing with each other was I a bitch. Or maybe I was a bitch then too but I was just too stupid to realize it. Things really have changed I see. Good-bye Tre. I won't bother you again."* I pressed end on my phone. I stood there for a while looking out at the cars passing. A part of me felt bad for carrying it with Lala the way that I had but how else was I supposed to treat her? She jumped up and left, not me. After all of these months of trying to do the right thing and get my relationship back on track with Kisha, I really didn't need Lala popping back up. Like my dad has always told me, the best way to handle the past is by leaving it in the past and that is exactly what I planned to do.

Lala

I sat in my car parked outside of my parent's house crying. I couldn't believe how Tre had just played me. Why was he being such an ass? I'd felt that it was a bad idea coming back home and contacting him. Honestly I'd felt like he might trip, though it never crossed my mind that he would be as cold as he'd been in his messages and then to top it off when I'd called he didn't answer.

I wiped my tears away with my hand. "Fuck Tre and fuck sitting here crying like some weak bitch! I don't need his ass! Me and my babies will be just fine without him!" As if they knew what I was saying I felt one of the baby's kick. I rubbed my belly. "That's right we don't need your stupid ass daddy! Mama will make sure that y'all are good! You can believe that!" I promised my babies. I sat there in the car for a little while before getting out and going back inside my parent's house. I'd been home for only a day now and my mama and daddy had been spoiling me ever since I'd walked through the door! My mama had called all of her friends and told them about my book. A few of them had even stopped by the day before and bought books from me, demanding that I autographed them! I would've given the books to them but they insisted on paying. Two of them bought more than one copy to give to other people. They were all so excited about me writing a book because no one from our small town had ever done anything like that before. The love and support that they'd showed made me feel really good and proud of myself.

When I walked inside the house the smell of food greeted me. I went into the kitchen and found my mama standing over the stove, stirring a pot. She glanced back at me as I took a seat at the table. "I am fixing your favorite! Cabbages seasoned with ham, baked chicken, macaroni and cheese, jiffy cornbread, and I bought a peach pie while I was out at the grocery store!"

My stomach growled just hearing her talk about all of the good food that she was cooking. I hadn't eaten ay of my mama's good cooking in a while. "I can't wait til' those cabbages get done!" She cooked the best cabbages!

She walked over to me and rubbed my belly. "Grandma is going to feed her little baby good while you're here!" I looked up at her and she was grinning from ear to ear. She was so excited about becoming a grandmother. My daddy was equally excited, that's all he'd talked about the night before.

"Ma, I can't be eating all of this good home cooking." I laughed. "I'm big enough now. By the time I leave here next week, I will have to be airlifted out of here!"

"Oh hush your mouth! You are going to feed my grandbaby, girl. You can worry about your figure after you have her." I'd told her that the baby was a girl. "You sure are big though. I don't know if you are going to make it another two months. You look like you are about to give birth now!"

"Yeah I know." I said taking a deep breath and then releasing it slowly.

"What's wrong?" Ma asked taking a seat in the chair next to me. "You seem like you have something on your mind. I've told you that you can talk to me about anything. I applaud you for being a strong woman and wanting to work through your problems on your own but there's nothing wrong with accepting a little help sometimes. Besides that's what I am here for, regardless of what it is." I looked at her, tears stinging the back of my eyes. The least little thing made me cry these days! She noticed the tears in my eyes. "What is it LaQuela?"

I ran my fingers through my hair, which now hung past my shoulders. "I'm just frustrated ma! It's like the harder I try to act like this situation doesn't bother me the more it does! I never thought that things would turn out this way but now that it has I don't know what to do! I thought that my leaving would solve everything but it didn't because no matter how far I run I can't run from my feelings for this man. I love him!" I cried. "I love him even more than I did before. Maybe it's because I am carrying his babies. I don't know what it is but I do know that there isn't a day that goes by where I do not think about him or think about all of the good times that we shared. I miss us laughing and joking around. I miss us sitting and talking for hours. Am I wrong for feeling the way that I do?" I looked at my ma waiting for an answer.

She reached over and caressed my face. "First of all stop that crying because it's not good for you or the baby."

"Ma, it's not only one baby...it's two." Her eyes grew huge. "I know...I didn't know how to tell you that it was twins at first but I am just so sick and tired of lying. I'm just tired!"

She shook her head and looked up towards the ceiling. "Lord have mercy, God give me the strength. Lala, is there anything else that you haven't told me that you need to tell me?"

"No ma'am."

"Girl, I am going to be honest with you. This is one messy situation that you have gotten yourself into! I mean it is just downright messy as can be! Now you asked me if you are wrong for feeling the way that you do. Baby you were wrong when you dropped your underwear and laid down with that man! What were you thinking? Were you thinking at all?"

"I don't know." I hung my head and looked down at my belly. "All I know is that now my babies aren't going to have a daddy and it's all my fault! I tried texting him and he told me not to text him anymore! I tried calling and he wouldn't answer. I left a voicemail telling him that I wouldn't bother him and anymore. I can't force him to see me or talk to me." I sniffled. There were so many emotions through me all at once. I felt lonely, stupid, confused, and hurt! I was just downright miserable at this point!

"What? Did you tell him that you are pregnant?"

"No, I want to tell him face to face not in a text or over the phone so that I can explain to him that is mostly the reason I left. I know how some men think and he may think that the babies aren't his. I have proof that I was pregnant before I left. My papers from my doctor have the date of conception on them. I brought them with me to show him if he acts like he doesn't believe me!"

Ma got up and went over to the stove to check her food. "Well you may just have to tell him over the phone if he won't agree to see you. Text him or leave a voicemail. One way or another he needs to know. I don't agree at all with how this happened because I feel like you could've went out here and found a man that didn't already have someone but the deed is done now and so I am not going to stand here and preach to you about what you should've done! Now all we can worry about is what you do from this point on."

"That's true." I agreed.

"So now what if you tell him and he says that he doesn't want anything to do with these babies. What are you going to do then?"

"I'm just going to raise my babies by myself. I'm not going to try and make this man be a part of their lives if he doesn't want to be!" Millions of women raised children by themselves every day! I could do it to if I needed to!

"Wrong!" She hit the counter with her hand! "You are going

to have these babies and make his ass take a paternity test! He may not want to be a daddy to them but he still has a responsibility to help take care of these children! As a mother your job is to make sure that these babies are well taken care of! Damn trying to look out for him! Look out for them! It's time that you put on your big girl panties and think like a grown woman! He played now it's time to pay! I have been listening to you talk about what you did and what you shouldn't have did and how you left so that you wouldn't cause him any drama! Hell he had a part in all of this! You didn't do all of this by yourself so you shouldn't take on all of the worry and responsibility by yourself! You are twenty-eight years old Lala! It's time that you start acting like it!"

"Why does everyone keep implying that I don't act my age?" I asked becoming agitated.

"Because you're not acting your age! A woman your age should know that when you play with fire you are bound to get burned! You want to play big girl games but then when things get tough you want to jump and run! Uh-uhh baby that ain't how you handle things like this! You stand up like a woman and meet this thing head on! I am not saying that you should go to his house and cause a scene or anything like that but don't back down and tuck your tail between your legs and go running back to Danville without doing what you came to do! If he doesn't want to meet you then that's fine, text him and let him know that you are pregnant! If he says that these babies aren't his then you tell him that you have proof. If he doesn't want to see it and still doubt you then you say okay and tell him that you and him can have a paternity test done after they are born! At this point you can't worry about protecting his relationship because to be perfectly honest it doesn't seem like he was too concerned about his relationship or family when he decided to have an ongoing relationship with you for two years behind his girlfriend's back! Let him worry about that situation and you worry about seeing to it that these babies are taken care of!"

Even though I knew the advice she was giving me was coming from a good place and that she was right. I still didn't want to cause Tre any drama. I know that I shouldn't give a damn about how things turned out for him as far as his girl was concerned after the way that he'd treated me when I'd reached out to him earlier but I did. I didn't want this to become a situation where things got ugly and we ended up hating each other and not being able to be civilized to each other. I felt like our situation could be handled in a civilized manner without a whole lot of drama. At the end of the day all I wanted was for him to at least be there for our babies. I knew that he couldn't be there full-time like I would love for him to be but as long as he did what he could I would be happy with that. Maybe we could even work this out to where his girl never found out and everybody could be happy...maybe.

Tre

When I got home it was a little after nine, the house was
quiet. I was a little tired, ready to take a hot shower and call it a
night. I still had Lala on my mind, wondering what she could
possibly want to talk to me about after all of this time. I laid my
keys down on the coffee table and walked down the hall to the
boy's room. I pushed the door opened and looked inside they were
both fast asleep. I went in and kissed both of them and put the
cover back on Shaun. He was a wild sleeper and always ended up
kicking his cover onto the floor sometime during the night. When I
was done I left out closing their door behind me. I continued down
the hallway to me and Kisha's bedroom. I pushed the door opened
and walked inside. I was expecting to find her already in bed

asleep or reading but to my surprise she was wide awake sitting in front of the computer.

She looked up from the computer as I walked into the room. "Hey baby!" She beamed excitedly. "Guess what?"

"Hey." I replied looking at her skeptically wondering what she was so excited about. "What's up?"

"Guess who I just sent a friend request to on Facebook?" She squealed and continued before I could answer. "LaQuela Chambers, the girl that wrote Confessions of A Side Chic! I am waiting for her to accept! I can't wait to tell her how much I enjoyed the book! There has to be a part two! I mean...I know damn well that Karma is going to get some revenge on Trent after he done got Lele pregnant!" She rattled on and on. I felt like I couldn't breathe. I kept thinking that maybe I'd heard her wrong or maybe she was talking about a different LaQuela Chambers. She had to be because there was no way in hell she was talking about Lala. I noticed her staring at me strangely. "Are you alright?"

"Yeah, I'm good." I said trying to pull myself together. I sat down on the edge of the bed. I needed a seat because my legs felt as if they were going to give out. Too much shit was coming at me all at once! "Baby, aren't you taking this book thing a little bit too far? You are a borderline stalker!" I was trying to play things off.

She twirled around in the desk chair that she was sitting in, cocking her head to one side and placing her hand on her hip. "Excuse you? Negro for your information, I am not nor will I ever be a stalker!" she corrected me. "I am friends with a lot of my favorite authors on Facebook! That is how I keep up with what they have going on and what they are about to drop next! This girl here is actually right from around here. I am really excited to know that we have an author from right here in Boykins…"

I didn't hear anything else that she said because now this shit had become too coincidental for it not to be Lala! I knew damn well there weren't two LaQuela Chambers from Boykins, VA. *Lala done wrote a fucking book?* I thought to myself and then I thought about the title…Confessions of A Side Chic! *Man what in the fuck is this crazy bitch trying to do? Is this what she wanted to talk to me about?*

"Tre…Tre!" Kisha called pulling me from my thoughts. "Tre did you hear anything that I just said?"

"Nah baby, my mind was somewhere else." I admitted truthfully. "What did you say?"

She smacked her lips and twirled her chair back around to face the computer. "Nothing…I didn't say anything!" She snapped. "That's just like you to have your mind somewhere else when I am talking to you!"

I placed my hand on her chair and turned her back around. "Yo, chill with the attitude and repeat what you were saying." I told her running my hand up her thigh, hoping to calm her down. It was just like her to get bent out of shape over something as little as a book. She just didn't realize the significance of what she had just dropped on me and I prayed that she never found out! "What were you saying?"

She moved her red and black braids out of her face, flipping them behind her shoulder. "I was saying that it's really dope to have someone from our small town write a book! Her information on Facebook says that she currently lives in Danville, VA but I was thinking that maybe she will come back to her hometown one day and do a book signing! That way I could meet her and get her to autograph my book! That shit would be so damn nice! I could say that I've actually met one of my favorite authors!"

I was looking at her like she'd lost her damn mind! If it were left up to me that shit was never going to happen! "Baby, you've only read one book from this chic! How in the hell does that make her one of your favorite authors?"

"Because Tre, the girl can write her ass off! She writes so that you actually feel like you can see everything as it is happening in the book! She definitely has a gift!" She bragged about Lala's book like a proud parent! "You wouldn't understand though because you are not a bookworm like myself." She giggled.

"Yeah, I guess you're right." I needed to find out more about this damn book. "So what was it about this book that made it so interesting that you are ready to go out and promote it?"

She smacked me on my arm playfully. "Whatever! I can't believe that you actually want to hear me talk about a book! Normally you be like, 'Bae, I don't want to hear that shit! That junk ain't real! You need to get your head out of them books and pay your man some attention!'" She mocked me.

She was right but this book right here was different because from the sound of the title it sounded like Lala was on some Karrine Steffans type shit! "When I don't want to listen you complain but when I show interest you complain as well. I can't win for losing with you woman."

"Well since you want to know, the book is about a guy named Trent who has been creeping on his girlfriend Karma with this chic named Lele. Him and Lele had been kicking it for two years when she found out that she was pregnant and left town, not letting Trent know anything about the baby. After she leaves she realizes just how much she loves him. She is torn between keeping the baby and raising it by herself and going back home and telling Trent the truth. She doesn't want him to think that she is trying to come between him and his girl but at the same time she wants him to know how she feels and about the baby that she is carrying. So after months of struggling with what she should do she goes back to her hometown and tells Trent about the baby. He of course is upset because he already has a girl and a family with her so he tells Lele that he doesn't want anything to do with her or her baby. It ended with Lele threatening to tell his girl Karma about their affair and her pregnancy!"

Man please, tell me that this shit is all just some shit that Lala made up! I thought to myself but my gut was telling me that this wasn't just a made up story! "Sounds like a soap opera to me." I told Kisha. I didn't want her to pick up on my uneasiness.

"I know right! That's what makes it so good! All of that drama has you fienin' for more! I can't wait until part two comes out to see what happens! I want Karma to whoop Lele's ass so bad because that heifer knew that Trent had a girl when she laid down with him!" Kisha continued on about the book. "I know triflin' bitches like that! Always after the next woman's man instead of finding their own! Then when the nigga don't want their asses no more they want to run tell his girl in hopes of breaking up their home because they are feeling some type of way. I hate bitches like that!"

"Kisha, it's only a book." I reminded her getting up and pulling my shirt over my head. I tossed my shirt on the chair that sat in the corner of the room. "I'm about to go take a shower."

"Alright baby." She turned back around to face the computer and I went into the bathroom.

In the bathroom, I turned on the water and adjusted it. I finished getting undressed and stepped in the shower under the hot water. As the hot water ran over my head I thought about the things that Kisha had just told me about Lala's book and about Lala's text messages from earlier. It didn't take a rocket scientist to figure out that Lala had based this book on me and her situation. The part that was fucking with me the most was the part about the character in the book leaving town because she'd found out that she was pregnant! I'd known all along that there was something that Lala wasn't telling me! Why in the fuck would she know she was pregnant and not tell me? She knew damn well I couldn't afford to have no baby with her! What in the fuck was I going to tell Kisha? How would Kisha react once she found out? So much shit was going through my head that it felt like my head was spinning! I washed up and got out of the shower. As I dried off I came to the conclusion that I needed to see Lala and this shit couldn't wait. I needed to see her that night! If she was pregnant there was no way that I was going to allow her to stay in Boykins! She was taking her ass back to Danville, her and her baby! I wasn't about to risk losing my family all because her feelings had gotten involved! Fuck that! She should've told me that she was pregnant instead of running off and deciding to keep a baby without discussing it with me like I didn't have any say in the matter! This bitch had definitely lost her mind!

I wrapped the towel around my waist and gathered my dirty clothes. I took everything that was in my pants pockets out and tossed my dirty clothes in the hamper. I opened the bathroom door and went back into the bedroom. I opened the drawer and took out a pair of basketball shorts and a t-shirt.

Kisha looked over at me, her eyebrows raised. "Where are you going?"

"Skeet just texted me and asked if I could give him a ride to Walmart. His daughter is sick and he needs to go and pick up some medicine." I lied. "I really don't feel like going but I know that he would do it for me."

She stared at me for a minute, while I slipped on my shoes. "Mmmmhmmm, don't let a trip to Walmart take your black ass all night Tre." She warned.

"Don't start." I replied calmly. I wasn't trying to argue with her.

"I'm not starting. I'm just letting you know."

I grabbed my keys and my phone and walked over to her kissing her on the lips. "I hear you baby."

"You better."

I left out of the house and hopped in my car. As soon as I got in the car I called Lala. It rang a few times and then her voicemail came on. I pressed end and then called back again, determined to reach her and get some answers as to what the fuck was going on! This time it rang three times before she picked up.

"Hello." She answered groggily.

"We need to talk. Meet me at the baseball park." I cut straight to the point. I didn't have time for a lot of small talk.

"Huh?"

I repeated myself, this time a little louder, not bothering to hide the irritation in my tone. "We need to talk. Meet me at the baseball park."

"Tre, it's almost 11:30. I am in the bed and I don't feel like getting up." She whined. "Can't this wait until tomorrow?"

I didn't give a fuck about her being in the bed or how she felt about getting up! My family was on the line! "Nah, it can't wait! Put on some clothes and meet me!"

I heard her smack her lips. "Give me about fifteen minutes! You got the nerve to call me with and attitude..."

I hung up the phone! I didn't want to hear that bullshit!

Lala

I took the phone from my ear and looked at it in disbelief. "I know that this motherfucka didn't just hang up on me!" I mumbled as I threw back the covers and tossed my phone onto the bed! I immediately became heated by the rudeness that Tre had displayed over the phone! I wasn't exactly sure where this attitude was coming from but we were about to straighten this shit once I saw him. I turned on the lamp by my bed and then went to the bathroom to empty my bladder. I also washed my face and brushed my teeth. When I was done I went back into my room to get dressed. I slipped my feet into my sneakers not bothering to put on any socks. I sat down on the bed and struggled to tie my shoes. At seven months I was huge and tying my shoes was more like a full body workout than a normal task. Once I had successfully accomplished tying my shoes I grabbed my keys and my phone and quietly headed out of the house locking the door behind me.

The warm summer air felt good. I jumped in my car and headed to the baseball park that was only ten minutes away. I was kind of nervous about seeing Tre after all of these months. I was nervous about his reaction once he saw that I was pregnant. I wondered what had changed his mind about wanting to see me. I didn't have to wonder long because minutes later I was turning into the park. I spotted him parked next to the fence. He was sitting on the hood of the car smoking a cigarette. I parked next to him and turned off the ignition and my lights. Instead of getting out of the car I rolled down the window.

Seeing him caused a flood of different emotions to run through me all at once. On the drive to the park my plan had been ready to check him about his attitude on sight but sitting there now face to face with him the only thing that managed to slip from my lips was, "Hey."

"Hey?" He snapped getting up from the hood of the car,

tossing the cigarette on the ground and walking over to my

window. "What the fuck do you mean, *hey*? What the hell is going

on with you?"

Just that quickly my anger returned. "Whoa…first of all you

need to check your shitty ass attitude with me! I don't know what

the fuck your problem is…"

"My fucking problem is you!" He roared. "I thought you had

bounced! So why in the fuck are you back? And what the fuck is

up with this book that I am hearing about? What you on some type

of slick ass Karrine Steffans type of shit?"

I was surprised to know that he had heard about my book so

quickly and shocked at the same time that he was comparing it to

Karrine's book! "What? What the fuck does my book have to do

with anything?" I questioned.

"It has a lot to do with everything because my girl read that

bullshit! Now she all on Facebook and shit sending you friend

requests and shit! Hollering about how good your book is! The shit

that is bothering me is that from what she was telling me about it the shit sounds a lot like our situation! I mean I ain't the smartest motherfucka but it doesn't take a gotdamn rocket scientist to figure out who the shit is based on!"

I sat there watching him spazz and it finally dawned on me why he had awakened me out of my sleep! "Oh I get it now, you are worried that ol girl is going to find out about us!" I chuckled sarcastically and sucked my teeth! "Well smart ass the only reason that you knew who it was based on was because you were a part of the situation! I am sure that everybody else who has read my book isn't sitting home saying '*Damn she is talking about her and Tre.*' Besides that it's a fictional story loosely based on us. I wrote the book because I was depressed about how things had turned out between us. It was sort of therapeutic for me because I was out there in Danville by myself. Once I started to write I saw that it was an interesting story and my friend that I met out there suggested I self-publish the book because she thought that it might sell. It turns out that she was right! I don't see why you are all bent out of shape about it! How is your girl going to find out that the book is based on us unless you tell her?"

This only seemed to piss him off even more! "You stupid bitch, are you listening to yourself? It isn't hard to connect the fucking dots!"

"Bitch?" I grabbed the latch on my door and flung it open. I jumped up out of the car and got in his face. "Nigga who are you calling a bitch?" I was so close that my stomach bumped him! "Was I a stupid bitch for the two years that you were fucking me? Nah nigga the bitch that was sitting at home waiting on you while your face was buried in my pussy was the stupid one!" Out of nowhere I felt stinging in the left side of my face! It took me a few seconds to realize what had just happened. I touched the side of my face where Tre had just slapped me! I looked up at him in disbelief.

"Yeah, I slapped your ass! You'd better watch your fucking mouth when you are talking about my girl!" He said glaring at me like he was daring me with his eyes to say anything else!

I looked up at him with tears in my eyes. "I know damn well

that you didn't just slap me!" I said still unable to believe what he had done. I lost it and started to swing on him like a mad woman!

He grabbed my arms and pinned me up against the car! "Go ahead now before I fuck you up out here!"

"I hate you!" I cried becoming emotional. "How are you going to stand here and put your hands on me? You come out here all mad with a fucked up attitude like I've done you wrong or something! Tell me Tre, what did I do to you?" I didn't allow him to answer. "I left! I left to keep from ruining your family because I knew that my feelings for you had become too strong for me to handle and because I knew that I was pregnant! I know how much Kisha and your boys mean to you so I put my own feelings aside and I walked away! I left everything so that you could keep everything! I left my job, my home and my family! I stayed in a fucking motel room for months! I was out there by myself without a fucking soul that I could depend on but myself! I did all of that so that you could keep your home! Do you have any idea what the fuck I have been going through? Do you even give a damn? Or are you so fucking selfish now that all you care about is Tre?"

He looked away and let go of my arms. "I can't lose my family." He stated calmly, rubbing the hair on his face. "I told you that from the start."

"Why are you acting like this is all my fault? I didn't make you do shit! You were a willing participant! If I remember correctly you were the one chasing me even after I told you no several times! Now all of a sudden you acting like some damn victim." I wiped my tears. "Don't worry, your girl won't find out. Especially not from me! I ain't that kind of bitch! I thought you knew me better than that but it's obvious that my judgment is all fucked up!" I opened my car door to get in. "By the way I'm seven months pregnant with twin girls and yes they are yours." I slid into the driver's seat and reached over in the glove box and retrieved the papers that I'd brought with me from my doctor and tossed them at him. "It's all good though. I see now that you don't want any parts of their lives and that's cool because honestly I don't want you anywhere around me or my babies!"

"Good! They probably ain't my babies anyways. Your whore ass probably don't know whose babies they are!" He spat.

"I'll be that motherfucka!" I started my car and put it in reverse. I sped out of the park leaving him standing beside his car. As I drove in the direction of my parent's house tears flowed freely down my cheeks. I was hurt by the scene that had just taken place but I'd learned a very valuable lesson from it all....karma is a bitch!

Tre

By the time I made it back home, it was a little after one. I dropped my keys down on the coffee table and walked down the hallway to my bedroom to let Kisha know that I was home. I pushed the door open and peeked inside. The room was dark and I could hear Kisha snoring softly. I eased the door shut and went back into the living room. I flopped down on the sofa and sat there in the dark letting the events that had taken place not too long ago play over in my head. I felt bad about putting my hands on Lala. I honestly felt like shit for that! My anger had managed to get the best of me and for a split second I lost control. I'd never put my hand on a woman before. The look in her eyes after I'd slapped her was such a pitiful sight. At the time I didn't care because she had made me so upset but thinking back on it, I felt horrible. I could have handled the situation a whole lot better than I had!

After she'd left I picked up the papers that she'd tossed at me and read over them. The papers confirmed her pregnancy and the conception date. Of course I didn't need confirmation that she was pregnant but the date of conception left no doubt in my mind that those were indeed my babies that she was carrying. *Damn what in the hell have I gotten myself into?* I thought to myself. *How in the hell am I going to tell Kisha that I've gotten some other chic pregnant with twins? She will never forgive my ass for this shit!* I sat up on the edge of the sofa with my head in my hands, a million thoughts running through my mind at once. I didn't want to lose my family. I had to figure out a way to fix this shit but as of right then I didn't see any way at all!

The next day I left home a little bit early so that I could go by Casper's crib and holla at him before heading to work. When I got there Tamika let me in.

"Hey, Tre." She greeted me as she opened the door and

stepped back to let me in. "Casper and Skeet are downstairs in the basement."

"Word." I responded walking past her.

"Tre..." She called after me. I stopped walking and looked back at her waiting to see what she wanted. She moved closer to me and I took a few steps back. "Ummm...I was wondering why you always be acting so uptight whenever I am around? You act like you don't like me or something. Is there a problem?"

This nasty bitch right here was a damn trip! "As a matter of fact there is a problem. I don't appreciate that shit that you did that night that I passed out down in the basement!" I replied trying not to talk too loud. "That was some foul shit! You did that shit right here in my man's crib like it wasn't nothing! You're a sorry bitch!"

She seemed unaffected by my words. She tucked her long weave behind her ear and looked up at me. "So are you telling me that you didn't like it? I mean, I could be wrong but judging from your moans I believe that you enjoyed it." She reached out and touched my chest. "You have no idea how long I've wanted you…"

I smacked her hand off of me, pointing my finger in her face. "Bitch what the fuck is wrong with you? You have the nerve to come at me like this after sitting your ass up in my house grinning in my girl's face! Look let's get something straight right now! I do not want your trifling nasty ass! Never have and never will! I don't see what Casper sees in you! Stay the fuck away from me and don't bring your ass back to my crib!"

She rolled her eyes. "Boy whatever, you trying to play like it's all me but I've caught you looking at my ass and shit! I don't know why you are frontin'. If you were so upset by what I did then why didn't you say something to Casper or tell Kisha?" she asked but didn't give me a chance to respond. "I'll tell you why because you liked that shit!"

I grabbed her by her face and pushed he head back roughly causing her to stumble a little. "Stay the fuck away from me!" I warned her before walking off. When I got downstairs, Skeet and Casper were playing the X-box and sharing a blunt. "What's good?" I greeted them walking over and giving each of them some dap before taking a seat.

"Ain't shit my nigga." Casper replied looking up from the game briefly. "What's good with you?"

"Bout to head to work in a few got a lot of shit on the dome though man." I admitted. "You got a beer?"

"Yeah over there in the refrigerator." He motioned towards the refrigerator sitting over in the corner. I got up and got me a beer. "Damn what in the hell you got going on that has you drinking before work and shit?"

I popped the top and drank half of the beer before responding. "Man, y'all remember the chic named Lala that I'd told y'all about that I was smashing for a minute?"

"Yeah." Skeet and Casper both nodded.

"Well y'all know that I told y'all that she packed up and dipped a while back. She had told me some shit about her being in love with me and not being able to continue to stay here and work with me. Well to make a long story short, she's back and seven months pregnant."

"Oh damn!" Skeet shook his head, pressing pause on the game controller and sitting it down. "Shit, it might not be yours! Don't fall for that shit man! Make that hoe prove it's yours before you get all worked up for nothing! Bitches be lying just to fuck your shit up! Does she know about Kisha?"

"Yeah..."

"Yeah that bitch probably lying, I agree with Skeet." Casper added. "Bitches ain't shit."

Just like the bitch you got laying up in your crib! I thought to myself. "There's more. She's pregnant with twins. She showed me the paperwork last night from her doctor. Judging by the conception date, they are my babies."

Skeet shook his head again. "Man if she was fucking you knowing that you already had a woman, there ain't no telling who else she was fucking! That bitch is probably a straight jumpoff! They could be anybody's babies!"

"Hell, yeah!" Casper laughed. "Shit, they may even be my

babies. How does she look? I may have smashed her." He and Skeet laughed.

"Yeah or they might be mines." Skeet joked. "Man, don't let that shit worry you. That hoe just wants some attention."

I decided to go ahead and tell them the rest. "She's written a book called Confessions of A Side Chic. The shit is about what happened between me and her. The worst part about it is Kisha done read the damn book and now she is Lala's biggest fan! She's all on Facebook trying to friend the bitch!"

Skeet threw up his hand. "Hold the fuck up! Did you just say that the bitch wrote a book about y'all? She didn't use your name did she?"

"Yeah she wrote a book and nah she didn't use my name. She used fake names."

"How the fuck did Kisha get the book?" Casper inquired.

"She ordered it. From what Kisha was telling me it's a huge success. You know how bitches are they love drama so the shit is probably selling like hotcakes!"

"Damn, I don't know whether to call this chic crazy or smart!" Skeet commented. "I mean at least she found a way to make some paper out of it all. Gotta give her credit for that but damn how many bitches are running around writing books about fucking the next bitch's man? Man, I don't know what type of bitch you done got yourself mixed up with."

"Well, how is she carrying shit? I mean, is she threatening to tell Kisha?"

I shook my head. "Nah, she isn't that type. She claims that the reason she left in the first place was because she didn't want to risk Kisha finding out. My question though is why in the fuck is she back now? If she stays here there is only a matter of time before Kisha finds out about this shit! You know Boykins is small as fuck and everybody is in everybody's business!"

"Well, why don't you sweet talk her into taking her ass back wherever she came from? You said that she was in love with you. Use that shit to your advantage! If she is in love with you then you can get her ass to do whatever you say. All you have to do is show her a little bit of attention from time to time and make her think that you love her ass too. I'll guarantee you that she won't tell shit and everything will be good. Just try to stay on the hoe's good side." Skeet suggested.

He did have a point that might just work. The only thing was that after the way that I had treated Lala the night before she may not want to hear shit that I had to say. "I don't know. I slapped her last night. She was talking out of the side of her neck and I lost it! I doubt if she wants anything else to do with my black ass. The last thing she said before she pulled off was, *I see now that you don't want any parts of their lives and that's cool because honestly I don't want you anywhere around me or my babies!* Then she left!"

"Well shit there you have it! If she doesn't want you anywhere around her or *her* babies then you have nothing to worry about." Casper said.

"But damn man, I feel bad about slapping her and if they are my babies. I ain't trying to be no deadbeat." I told him.

"I feel you on that." Skeet agreed. "But it's either that or lose Kisha and your boys because you know damn well that if Kisha finds out about this shit, it's going to be a wrap!"

"I know."

"It's a lot to think about but give it a few days. Give this girl a few days to cool off and then call her up and try to persuade her to leave town again. It will be a lot easier for you to deal with the situation without her being in the same small ass town with you and your girl. You have a better chance of Kisha not finding out."

"Yeah that's true." I finished my beer and took a look at my watch. "Let me get my ass up out of here and go punch this damn clock. Umma holla at y'all niggas a little bit later. I sure appreciate y'all listening to a nigga and trying to help me straighten this shit out."

"No problem my nigga, that's what we are here for." Casper assured me.

"Yeah we are here to help your ass sort through this damn real-life soap opera that you got going on!" Skeet laughed. "I bet you'll keep your dick in your pants from now on!"

"Shit…and you ain't know? Trust me I have learned my lesson!" I gave each of them some dap before turning to leave. On my way up the basement steps, I bumped directly into Tamika.

"Bye Tre…" She smirked. "You have a good day now."

"Fuck you…" I mumbled under my breath and continued up the stairs.

When I pulled into the parking lot of Service Master, I noticed Lala's car parked next to one of the company vans. "What in the fuck is she doing here?" I asked aloud as I gathered my things and got out of my car.

Lala

After seeing Tre the night before and thinking over how he'd treated me. I'd decided that it was time to stop trying to be nice and worrying about protecting a motherfucka who obviously didn't give a damn about me. I was more than a little hurt by Tre's reaction and especially the fact that he'd put his hands on me. After dealing with him for over two years this was how he was going to treat me? No one could have ever told me that things would turn out this way. This man wasn't the man that I'd been having a relationship with for the past two years. He was somebody else or maybe he'd been this way all along. I'd just never seen this side of him but when shit gets hot people normally show their true colors! It's cool though because I was about to show him another side of me as well. He was going to wish that he'd seen my red ass and ran in the other direction!

I'd decided to wait for Tre at his job. When I saw his Charger pull into the parking lot of Service Master, I mumbled. "Game time motherfucka!" I got out of my car and walked over to his.

He pressed the button on his keychain remote to lock his car doors and activate the alarm before turning to acknowledge me. "What are you doing here Lala?" His tone was much calmer than it had been the night before. He looked as if he hadn't had much sleep. Oh well he was about to lose a whole lot more!

"I came to see you. Don't worry I won't take up much of your time." I assured him. "I did some thinking last night after I left you. I realized that I have more than gone out of my way to be good to you but in return all I got was shitted on..." He got ready to say something but I held up my hand to silence him. "I'm not finished! I can understand your frustration and everything given the situation but the way that you handled things last night was dead wrong! So now I'm done being nice! From this moment on I don't give a fuck about your relationship or nothing else! Why should I give a fuck? For two whole years you didn't give a fuck but now you want to play victim like you were raped! Well you can play it however you want but here is how I am going to play it! When I give birth to these babies, I am going to slap a paternity test on your ass and then I am going to dig into this Service Master check! I'd advise you to start looking for another job because your ass is going to need it!" After saying my piece I turned to walk away but he grabbed me by the arm and spun me back around.

"Wait a minute! Are you threatening me?" He snarled.

I snatched my arm away from him. "No motherfucka I am promising you! Don't put your hands on me again or else you will also have to worry about coming up with bail money!" I warned. "I tried to be nice to you but you didn't want it that way so now fuck you!" I headed to my car.

"Oh so now it's like that? When you get mad you want to threaten a nigga?" he followed me.

"Tre save that bullshit for somebody who actually wants to hear it! I sure as hell don't! Your only concern is your selfish ass self! You don't give a damn about me, my babies or your family at home if you ask me!" He grabbed me again, turning me around to face him. He held onto both of my arms so tightly that it hurt. "Let go of me!"

"Fuck that! Lala, I am not going to lose my family for you and nobody else! I mean that shit! Why can't you just go back to Danville where you were? We can work out something as far as me helping you with the babies but all of this paternity shit that you are talking about ain't going down!"

I looked him dead in the eyes and burst out laughing. "Ooooh so now we can work something out? Now you want to be civilized? Hmmm…let me think about that for a second." I rolled my eyes up in my head pretending to think for a second. "Ummmm…nope! Now who's the stupid bitch? You thought that you could treat me the way that you did and then expect for shit to still be good? Nigga you must be smoking! Now turn me a loose!" I can't lie looking up into those brown eyes of his was making me a little weak but I kept reminding myself of how he had treated me the night before and remained strong.

He tightened his grip and spoke through clenched. "What you think this shit is a game? Bitch…I mean girl this is my fucking family that you are playing with! What do you expect to gain from this bullshit?"

"Right now I expect for you to take your hands off of me!" I snapped.

"Excuse me but is everything alright over here?" A familiar voice asked from behind Tre.

Tre let go of me and turned around. Mr. Johnson was standing there waiting for an answer. "Yeah everything is straight." Tre answered.

"Lala are you okay?" He asked looking from Tre to me skeptically.

"Yes sir everything is fine." I smiled. "Tre and I were just talking."

"Alright, I didn't know what was going on. I saw you two through the window and things looked a bit heated. I just wanted to make sure that everything was fine."

"Yes sir, I understand and I appreciate that."

"No problem. How have you been? I see that you've been eating good." He joked nodding towards my belly.

I laughed. "Yeah I have been eating pretty good." I played along.

"How far along are you?" He asked.

"Seven months and I will be glad when it's over.'

"Well congratulations. I sure do miss having you around here. You were one of my best workers."

"Awww...thank you. I miss you too Mr. Johnson."

"I don't know your reason for leaving but if it had anything to do with your pregnancy you could've come and talked to me. I would've found something else for you to do."

"That was one of the reasons." I admitted. "But there were a few other personal things as well." I glanced at Tre briefly.

He scratched his head. "I see, well listen here if you ever want to come back after you have your baby just let me know.

There's always a place for you here." He patted me on the arm.

Tre looked like he wanted to choke the hell out of the both of us. "Thank you so much. I will keep that in mind." I looked at Tre and smirked.

"Alright then it was great seeing you again. Take care and congratulations again." He gave me a hugged and then went back inside the building.

"I guess I'd better be going. I'll be in touch." I told Tre as I opened the door to get inside my car.

"Lala, this conversation isn't over. We need to come to some type of agreement."

"Bye Tre." I closed my door and started the ignition.

"This shit isn't funny yo."

"I agree and it's about to get even less funny real soon." I put my car in reverse and left him standing in the parking lot. I couldn't help but burst into laughter as I thought about the helpless expression on his face. "That's what you get for fucking with a bitch like me!"

A few minutes past before my phone vibrated alerting me that I had a new text message. I picked up my phone and checked the message. **Tre: We need to talk once both of us have calmed down and are thinking clearly.**

Me: Boy bye…stop texting my fucking phone…remember that? It's funny how your words can come back to bite you in the ass isn't it? After replying I turned off my phone and tossed it in the passenger seat.

When I got back to my parent's house I packed up my things so that I would be ready to head back to Danville the next morning. I'd handled my business here for the time being and now it was time for me to head home. I was missing Nisey and Evan terribly and also ready to leave Boykins.

Later that night as me and my parents sat in the living room eating some of my mom's homemade apple pie with vanilla ice cream. My dad asked. "So have you talked to the babies' father?"

"Yes sir, I have."

"And…what did he say? Is he going to help you with them?"

"Yeah." I lied, well not really because he was going to help. Maybe not by choice but he was definitely going to help. "Yeah everything went well."

"That's good." My ma commented. "I thought he was going to be a bit of a problem being that he's already living with a woman. How is he going to tell her about you and the babies?"

"I have no idea. That's his problem not mine." I answered truthfully. "I really don't want to talk about this on my last night here. I just want to enjoy the two of you."

"Alright baby." My ma agreed. "You know, I really don't like the idea of you driving back by yourself. You are too far along to be traveling long distances alone. I know you aren't due for another month or so but anything could happen."

I hadn't given that any thought at all but I was sure that everything would be fine. My parent's worried way too much. "I'll be fine ma."

"Lala, your mama is right. Maybe you should let me take you back or you could stay here."

"No, I couldn't ask you to do that. And what about my car? If you took me back how am I supposed to get my car?"

"Or you could stay here." He repeated.

"No daddy, I have to go back."

"Why do you *have* to go back?"

"Because that's where I live now." I laughed. "I will be fine and if anything happens I have my cell."

"Baby, I don't know about you traveling alone…" My ma said again. "I will just be worried to death the entire time."

"Ma, I will be fine." I assured her.

"Alright Lala, but call me every hour to let me know that you are okay."

"I will…I promise." We sat and talked for a while longer before I decided to go to bed. I kissed both of my parents and told them I loved them because I was sure that they would both be asleep when I left in the morning.

I took a hot shower and then got in bed. After laying down I remembered that I had turned off my cell earlier. I got up and got my cell from my pocketbook and turned it back on so that I could set the alarm to wake me in the morning. No sooner than I powered on my cell a flood of text messages came through. There were several from Tre telling me that we needed to talk and one from Nisey telling me that she couldn't wait to see me and how much she missed me. I also had a voicemail notification. I dialed my voicemail and typed in my pin. Tre's voice poured through the phone, *"Lala, this shit has gotten way out of hand. I apologize for putting my hands on you last night. That shit wasn't cool. I was just frustrated. I mean, first you up and leave without telling me anything. Now you're back and I hear that you've written this book and you're pregnant! It's just a lot for a nigga to digest all at once. I understand that you are mad but shit doesn't have to be this way. You and I are better than this. Also you were right when you said that you've been more than nice by leaving and not causing me any problems. Not just that but you put your own feelings to the side for me. I appreciate that because you could've done like most bitches and caused a lot of drama but you didn't. Well I'm going to get off this phone but I would appreciate it if you would call me*

back so that we can talk and come to some kind of agreement.

Alright holla back." With that he disconnected the call.

I sat there on side of my bed holding the phone with tears

streaming down my face. *Now why couldn't he have just done that*

to start with? I wondered. All I'd wanted from the beginning was

for him to be civilized. I looked at the time on my phone. It read

10:21pm. I strolled through my call log until I came to Tre's name

and then pressed send. The phone rang a few times before he

answered.

"Hello."

"Hey." I sniffled. "What do you want to talk about?"

"Are you crying?" There was unexpected concern in his tone.

"What's wrong?"

"Nothing." I replied using my hands to wipe my tears away.

"What's up?"

He ignored my question and asked. "What do you mean

nothing? Something is obviously wrong if you are crying."

I let out a sigh. "I'm just very emotional due to the pregnancy and listening to your message made me cry. Tre, I don't want to fight with you. That is not at all why I came here. I just wanted you to know about the babies because I felt you deserved to know."

I heard him let out a sigh as well. "I feel you but listen I am at my last building. I should be done within the next hour. I am in Suffolk tonight so I should be back at the Service Master building no later than 12:30 or 1:00. Do you think we could meet there and talk when I get off?"

"Yeah but I can't stay long because I am leaving early in the morning to go back home."

"Alright, I'll see you then. I'll call you when I am almost there."

"Okay." We hung up and I laid down to get a nap in before I had to go and meet Tre. Not too long after dozing off I, woke up to my phone ringing and having sharp pains in the bottom of my stomach. They weren't unbearable but they were painful enough. I grabbed my phone and answered it.

"Hey, I'm almost at Service Master." Tre said as soon as I answered.

"Okay, I'll be there."

"Alright…" We hung up and I got up, went into the kitchen and got a glass of water. Then I went into the bathroom and got the Tylenol out of the medicine cabinet and took two. I went back to my room and got dressed, then left to go meet Tre.

Tre

On the drive back to Service Master I was happy as fuck to know that Lala had calmed down. I knew without a doubt that I could change her mind about the paternity and child support shit that she'd been yapping about earlier. I'd known that she'd said all of it out of anger but I'd also known that there was no way in hell that I could let her go through with it because there was no way in hell that I could possibly hide all of that shit without Kisha finding out. I knew that when I talked to her I had to choose my words carefully so that I wouldn't set her off again. As long as I kept her happy I had a chance at keeping this shit quiet.

I pulled into the parking lot at Service Master and parked next to my car. Lala hadn't arrived yet, so I turned on the radio and sat in the van and waited. A few minutes later Lala pulled up and parked next to me. I got out of the van and walked over to her car. She unlocked the door and I got in on the passenger side. She looked really tired. For the first time, I took a minute to really look at her. Her hair had grown a lot in the past few months and even though she'd put on a lot of weight due to the pregnancy she was still beautiful as ever. I had to admit she looked really cute pregnant.

"Hey." She spoke first.

"Hey. I know it's late and you're tired so I won't hold you long." I told her. "Look I want to apologize again for putting my hands on you." She didn't say anything she just nodded her head. "Why didn't you tell me that you were pregnant before you left?"

"Honestly, I didn't know how to tell you. I was afraid. I knew that you wouldn't be too happy about it because of your situation and I assumed that you would more than likely ask me to get an abortion. I wasn't sure if that was what I wanted. I didn't really decide to keep what I thought was one baby until after I had left. I just couldn't bring myself to have an abortion. I figured that I would just keep the baby and raise it by myself. Of course when I found out later that I was pregnant with twins, I thought that maybe I should've went ahead and got an abortion because two babies were going to be a lot more responsibility than what I had planned for. Then I realized that regardless of whether it was one or two they were still mine and it would have been fucked up for me to kill them because of the fucked up choices that I made."

I nodded my head. "So what made you decide to come back and tell me now?"

"Well my parents and my friend Nisey convinced me to tell you. They felt like you had the right to know and then decide whether or not you wanted to be a part of the babies lives or not. If it were left up to me, I probably wouldn't have ever told you but the more I thought about what they were saying. I figured they had a point. I would want to know if I had a child or children somewhere out here in the world if I were a man. I would want the mother to give me the opportunity to make my own decision as to whether or not I wanted to be a part of my child's life or not."

I sat up and placed my head in my hands. "Fuck! This right here is crazy!" I knew that I couldn't blame this all on her. I couldn't even be mad at the fact that she hadn't gotten an abortion. She had the right to choose to keep the babies but this just wasn't a good situation for me. Regardless of how long I hid this shit from Kisha it was bound to come out sooner or later. I couldn't hide two damn kids and another babymama forever! I sat back up and looked over at Lala. "I have to ask you this and I hope that you don't take this the wrong way. But are you sure those are my babies?"

She let out a sarcastic chuckle and shook her head. "Nigga are you serious? Are you really sitting here asking me this shit?" She screamed banging her hand on the steering wheel! "Before I left you and I both know it was all about you! I didn't even have time to fuck with another nigga because every minute that you got away from Kisha we were together. No matter what time you called day or night I was always available! So when did I have time for another nigga Tre?"

I saw her getting upset so I tried to defuse the situation before it got out of hand. "Calm down Lala…"

"No fuck that! I am sick of you treating me like I'm some hoe! I haven't been with anyone but you! You and only you! I can't even imagine fucking with another man! Do you know why? Huh?"

I knew she wanted me to ask so I did. "Why?"

"Because I love you…" Her voice cracked and the tears began to roll. "I know that you don't love me or even have feelings for me but that doesn't change the way that I feel about you. I missed you so much when I was away that it hurt. I missed laughing with you and us talking for hours about any and everything. I missed you making love to me, the way that your body felt against mine, how your lips felt on my skin, the way that you smell, and the way that you taste…I missed everything. I just missed you…us. You have no idea what I have been going through since that day that I left. I not only lost my lover but I lost my friend. People from the outside looking in can judge me and say that I ain't shit because I fell in love with and got pregnant by another woman's man but all of those people can kiss my red ass. Those people don't know how you made me feel when I was with you. It wasn't just about sex with us. It was something much deeper than that. I wish that we could have met under different circumstance but fuck it…shit happens. I don't regret being with you and if I had to do it all over again…I would."

Hearing her pour her heart out to me like that did something to me. Before I had a chance to think about what I was doing I leaned over and covered her lips with mine. We kissed like two long lost lovers. I can't say how long the kiss lasted but Lala was the first to pull back. She grabbed her stomach and grimaced like she was in pain.

"What's wrong?" I asked unconsciously touching her belly.

"Nothing…just had a little pain that's all. I'm fine." She assured me but the look on her face was saying something different.

"Are you sure that you are okay?" I asked removing my hand

from her stomach.

"Yeah, I'm good." She took my hand and placed it back on her stomach. "Don't move it." She looked at me with those beautiful green eyes that had trapped my ass in the beginning. She leaned over and kissed me again. I kissed her back enjoying the taste of her lips and tongue. I knew that I was dead wrong for what I was doing. The point of me coming here had been to try to come to some type of resolution to the shit that my dick had already gotten me into but instead I was making it even worst. My hand found its way underneath Lala's shirt. I caressed her swollen breasts through her bra. I heard her let out a soft moan. I let go of her lips and kissed a trail down her neck.

"Mmmmm…Tre, I've missed you so much. Make love to me…please." Lala begged.

My dick was rock hard and standing at attention. I believe I wanted her just as bad or more than she wanted me at this moment. It had been a long time since I'd sampled her sweet punany. I stopped kissing and nibbling her neck long enough to respond.

"There isn't enough room in here. We are going to have to move to the van."

"I don't care where we have to move to. Hell right now we could move on the ground. I haven't had any since the last time we were together. My body is long overdue."

Without further discussion we got out of her car and moved to the van. Once we were inside I undressed her from waist down and myself. "Are you comfortable?" I asked her.

"Not really but I'll be alright." She responded as she turned on her side.

"I remember the first time that you let me taste it was in the back of this van." I reminded her as I kissed up her thigh.

"I wish that you'd stop teasing me and taste it now."

"Turn around."

She got up on all fours and I got behind her. I used my hands to spread her ass cheeks giving me an open view of her beautiful pink pussy. I didn't waste any time diving in. I licked and sucked on her clit for less than a minute before she started to scream and holler while her legs shook uncontrollably. "Oh shit Tre!" I sat up and smiled. It was just like old times when I used to make her cum with little or no effort!

"Mmmm…you know that I ain't finished yet." I put my face back where it had just come from and brought her to another powerful orgasm before entering her from behind. I took my time and stroked her nice and slow. I didn't want to hurt her. The way that her muscles gripped my dick sucking me in deeper should have been against the law! She was so wet that her pussy was talking to me! "Damn baby this pussy is good." I growled.

"Mmmm…you missed this pussy didn't you, daddy?" She asked as she threw her hips back to meet my thrusts.

"Fuck yeah…I missed this shit girl." I leaned over and planted kisses on her back as I continued to grind deep inside of her. I felt my orgasm building and I picked up the pace a little.

"Ooowww…Tre…slow down!" Lala squealed. I was in a zone as I continued to pump faster until I exploded inside of her. "Ooouuccch! Fuck! Tre…that shit hurt!" She had one had behind her pushing in my stomach trying to push me away.

"I'm sorry...baby." I apologized as I collapsed on top of her sweating and trying to catch my breath. I had forgotten just how good her pussy was. "Damn girl..."

"Move so that I can get up!" Lala snapped. "You going all crazy like you ain't got no sense! I told you that mess hurt!"

I smacked her on the butt before moving so that she could get up. "I said that I was sorry. I didn't mean to hurt you but it wasn't my fault."

"Who's was it then?" She asked getting dressed.

"Yours cuz your stuff shouldn't be so good." I laughed as I slipped on my boxers and shorts. After we were both done getting dressed I helped her out of the back of the van and then walked her back over to her car.

"So what are we going to do?" She asked leaning back against the car and looking up at me.

"I am going to keep in contact with you after you go back and then once the babies are born I am going to start sending you money every two weeks to help you out. I am going to send you something next week to help get whatever you might need for them before they get here." I reached out and rubbed her belly.

"That's all good but what about you seeing them or possibly being there when they are born?"

"I'm going to try and see them when I can even if you and I have to meet up half way or something. We'll work something out when the time comes." I assured her. "Now as far as me being there when they are born…I can't promise you that. You know my situation now. I can try my best but you and I both know that I am not going to be there like you want me to be or even how I want to be."

I could tell by the expression on her face that she wasn't really happy with my response but instead of putting up a fuss she just simply said. "Okay."

"Alright well I am going to let you go so that you can get some rest before you hit the road in the morning. Even though we haven't quite seen eye to eye for the most of your visit, I am glad that we were able to come to an understanding before you left." I pulled her into my arms. "Take care of yourself and my babies and I will be in touch. As a matter of fact call me and let me know that you made it back safely."

"I will." She looked sad.

I kissed her on her forehead before releasing her and then opened her car door for her. She got inside and I closed the door. I stood there and watched her until she was out of the parking lot. I got in my car and headed home. One babymama taken care of at least for the time being...

Lala

I really wasn't ready to leave Tre but I knew that he had to go home. I was glad that we had come to some type of agreement. I knew that his reasons for being nice to me and deciding to act civilized were more so to benefit him than anything. I knew that he was trying to keep me happy so that I wouldn't slap a paternity test on his ass or child support! He wasn't fooling anyone but I was willing to deal with that for now. Even through all of the bullshit that he'd just thrown my way to make me happy, one thing was for certain. There was still an undeniable chemistry between the two of us, Kisha may have had his heart but somewhere in there he possessed some feelings for me. They may not have been as deep as my feelings for him but they were there.

When I got home it was a little after 3:00, I took a quick

wash up and went straight to bed. I was still having pains in the bottom of my stomach so I tossed and turned for a little while before I was able to fall asleep. My alarm went off at 5:30, I turned over and cut it off and then went back to sleep. When I woke up again it was 7:15. I got up and got dressed, I was still having a few pains in the bottom of my stomach but they weren't as bad as they'd been before. I figured it was just Braxton Hicks. My dad had taken my things out to the car the night before so I grabbed my pocketbook and closed the door to my room. The smell of food invaded my nostrils as I made my way down the long hallway. I sat my pocketbook down on the sofa and went into the kitchen. My dad was sitting at the table having his morning cup of coffee and my ma was fixing plates.

"Good morning baby." My dad looked up at me as I entered the kitchen.

"Good morning." I replied taking a seat at the table. "What are you two doing up?"

My ma placed a plate with fried apples, turkey bacon, cheesy eggs, grits and biscuits in front of me. "Now you know goodness well that we weren't going to allow you to leave here without seeing you off! Plus I had to feed grandmama's little boogers!" She rubbed my stomach.

I giggled. "Thanks ma." I bowed my head and said my grace before digging into my food. "Ma, I cannot eat all of this food. You do know that right?"

"All that you don't eat I will put it in a Tupperware plate for you to take with you, no big deal." She placed a plate in front of my dad and then fixed her own plate and sat down.

"Are you sure that you don't want me to drive you back, Lala?" My dad asked.

"I'm sure daddy. I'll be fine."

He let out a sigh and placed his fork in his plate. "Girl, I tell you. You are just like your mama when you get your mind set one way that's it. There's no use in trying to change it. You don't need to be out there on that road by yourself as far along as you are girl!"

I seriously didn't feel like arguing with him. "Daddy, I will be fine. I have my phone in case anything happens and I promised that I would call you two every hour. Stop worrying so much...okay?"

"Alright." He shook his head, picking up his fork he continued to eat.

After we were done eating my ma packed me a to-go plate and then her and my dad walked me out to my car. I gave them both hugs and kisses and then I got in my car and headed back to Danville.

Two hours into my drive, the pains in my stomach had gotten worse. They were so bad that I had tears in my eyes. There was no way that I could continue to drive so I got off on the first exit that I saw stopped at the first little store that I saw, it didn't look like it got much business. The only way that I knew it was open was because of the neon sign in the window that said open. I parked and leaned my head back against the seat and closed my eyes. I didn't bother to turn off the ignition because it was pretty warm and I needed to keep the AC running. I leaned the seat back a little. "Whew lord please let these pains go away." I prayed. I thought about calling my parents but I didn't want to worry them if it was only Braxton Hicks. Plus I didn't feel like hearing them fuss because they had warned me about driving back alone. I sat there with my eyes closed for a few minutes before there was a tap on my window. I opened my eyes and look to see who it was. There was a tall muscular brother with skin the color of dark milk chocolate standing outside of my car.

I rolled down the window. "Hey."

"Hey there…I came out to see if you were alright." He asked in a thick country accent.

"Yeah…I'm fine." Sweat had begun to pour from my pores and the pains were getting sharper. "Oh jesus!" I screamed as another pain came.

"Ma'am, you don't look alright." The man said looking at me wearing a concerned expression.

"I think…I may be going into labor…but I'm not due for

another month and a half."

His expression went from concerned to scared. "Shit! Ummm... are you from around here?"

"No, I am from Boykins, VA but I live in Danville. That's where I am headed now."

"Where's your boyfriend or husband? I could call him for you?" He offered.

"Don't have either."

"Well what about your family? There has to be someone that I can call for you."

A pain hit me and I had to grab ahold of the steering wheel! I tried breathing the way that I'd been taught in the one Lamaze class that I'd gone to but that shit wasn't working. When the contraction finally subsided, I was able to answer. "I'll call my parents. Thank you but you don't have to stay out here with me. I'll be fine."

"I know I don't have to but I wouldn't dare leave you out here alone like this. Where are your parents?"

"In Boykins."

He looked at me like I had lost my mind. "In Boykins? Woman that is like two hours and some change away! You can't sit here that long and wait on them! I have to get you to a hospital! I don't know much about having no babies but I do know that you can't just sit here and chill."

"I'm..." Another contraction came and then I felt like I'd just peed on myself. I panicked, "Omigod...I think my water just broke!"

"Huh? Okay...hold on. I'm going to call the ambulance for you." He took out his cell and called the ambulance and told them the situation and gave them the address to where we were.

I grabbed my cell and called my parents. The phone didn't ring but once before my ma answered. "Girl, I was just..."

"Ma, I'm in labor." I blurted between contractions.

"What? Oh my goodness. Baby, where are you?"

"I'm in South Boston, VA. It's a small town before you get to Danville." I informed her.

"I know where it is." I heard her yell to my daddy. "Earl, we have to go! We have to go right now! Lala done went into labor out on the road! I knew something like this was going to happen! I knew it! That's why I didn't want her out there by herself! Lord please protect my baby until I can get to her." Her voice cracked. I knew that she was worried sick.

"Ma, I am not on the road. I am at a store." I tried to comfort her by assuring her that I was fine. "There's a nice man here with me. He has called the ambulance for me and they are on the way."

"What is the name of the hospital that they are taking you to?"

I took the phone from my ear. "Sir, can you tell me the name of the hospital that they will be taking me to?"

"Yes, ummm…Halifax Regional."

I repeated what he'd said to my mama. "Alright we are on our way. You hang up and try to stay calm and breathe. I know that you are in a lot of pain but it will all be over soon and you will be holding those two beautiful princesses in your arms."

"Okay ma…I'll talk to you in a few." I hung up and texted

Tre. **I'm in labor. Call me asap!!!**

Tre

I woke up the next morning to help get the boys ready for

school. As I helped them get dressed I thought about Lala and the

babies that she was carrying and what it would be like knowing

that I had two other children in the world that I wasn't there for. I

wasn't sure if I could live with myself if I turned my back on my

own flesh and blood. I hadn't been raised that way. I'd done a lot

of shit in my life and in my relationship but the one thing that I

always took pride in was being a father to my children. I watched

Quan and Shaun as they stood at the sink and brushed their teeth.

There was nothing in the world that I wouldn't do for my two little

men. I knew that I'd done the right thing by talking to Lala, now

all I had to do was make this shit work. Even though I didn't want

to risk losing my family, I also didn't want to risk missing out on my daughter's lives either. They didn't deserve that and to keep it one hundred Lala didn't deserve to have to worry about raising them all by herself either. She wouldn't have to though because regardless of what had to do and how many lies I had to tell to cover my ass I was going to be there for my seeds.

"Baby, I was thinking that you and I could go out for breakfast after we put the boys on the bus." Kisha walked into the bathroom interrupting my thoughts. "What do you think?"

"Yeah, we can do that." I agreed. I felt a little bit guilty as I stood there looking at her knowing all of the shit that I was hiding and that I'd just been unfaithful to her again just a few hours ago. I was definitely playing with fire!

"I'm finished daddy." Quan announced running over to me. "Smell my breath! I brushed really good!"

"Me too! Smell mines too!" Shaun was right behind him.

I leaned down and gave them both the sniff test. "Good job fellas!" I gave them both a high-five. They ran out of the bathroom and headed in their room to grab their backpacks. "Y'all hurry up now. The bus will be here in a few."

Kisha wrapped her arms around me and stood on her tiptoes to give me a kiss. I gave her a light peck on the lips. I really wasn't in the mood for kissing. I had too much on my mind. If she knew the shit that I'd done the last thing on her mind would be kissing. "What's wrong baby?" She asked looking up at me.

"Nothing." I lied running my hands down her back and then lower to palm her round backside. I gave it a light squeeze. "Everything is good."

"Okay well I am going to go get dressed." She gave me another peck and then went into the bedroom to get her clothes. I went down the hall to check on the boys. They were in their room playing with their toys.

"Time to go outside and wait for the bus…let's go." I told them. They grabbed their backpacks and we went outside.

After the boys got on the bus I went back inside took a quick shower and then got dressed. Kisha wanted to go to the Huddle House for breakfast which was like a twenty minute drive from where we lived. On the drive there she talked nonstop about random stuff. I didn't hear most of what she was saying because I was too wrapped up in my own thoughts. Every now and again I would nod my head like I was paying attention.

We were seated in a booth near the window enjoying blueberry waffles and turkey sausage when Kisha put down her fork and looked up at me. "Baby, I was thinking that maybe we could go ahead and get married in like the next six months." She smiled. "I'm ready. Aren't you? I mean we don't have to have anything big just a small intimate get together with our closest family and friends."

Getting married was totally out of the question right now until I saw how this arrangement was going to work out with Lala. I knew that if I told her that I didn't think that it was a good idea or that I wasn't ready it would more than likely lead to an argument. So I decided to use a different approach. "Baby, I was hoping that we could move into a bigger place before we get married. I want a house, somewhere where the boys have a big backyard to play in.

You know something really nice. Maybe we could look into renting to own."

She rolled her eyes. "Tre what does us getting married have to do with us getting a house? What you done changed your mind about us getting married?"

"See there you go! That's not what I said. Why do you always have to turn shit around and make more out of it than what it is? We can't afford to do both right now. A wedding costs money Kisha regardless of how big or small it is. I say we move first and then do the wedding later. We might be able to even do the wedding in the backyard at our house."

She rolled her eyes again. "Tre a wedding won't cost that much! Dag you acting like we about to have some big fancy wedding! I just want something simple! That's it!" She folded her arms and leaned back in her chair.

"Have you forgotten that we have bills and shit and that I am the only one working? We just can't afford it right now!" I stressed to her. Even though I really wasn't ready to get married the things that I was pointing out to her was real. We really couldn't afford to have a wedding. Especially not with me having two more babies on the way! Shit I already knew I was going to need to start looking for a new job soon and to keep it real her getting a job wasn't a bad idea either. I know that may seem fucked up being that I was the one who got somebody else pregnant but it was what it was! This shit just seemed to get worse and worse. Every time that I thought I had shit half way under control something else came up!

She sat up. "Nigga what are you trying to say? You were the one who said that you didn't want me to work and that you would rather I stay home and take care of the boys. I could've been gotten a job!"

"Kisha, all I am saying is that we can't afford it right now. Why are you making such a big deal about nothing? I didn't say that we couldn't get married. I just said not right now…"

"You're always saying not right now!" She snapped. "I'm getting sick of this shit right here! I ain't shacking forever! I've been doing it long enough so you need to get your shit together like asap!"

I was about to respond when my cell vibrated. I took it out of the clip and looked at it. I didn't recognize the number but the message read: **You should be more careful when telling your business. You never know who could be standing around the corner listening or recording your conversation.**

I looked at my phone confused before responding. **Me: Wtf? Who is this and wth are you talking about?"**

Anonymous: Lol I'm talking about the author hoe that you got pregnant! I wonder what would happen if Kisha found out about your side bitch? I guess I wasn't good enough for you...

Tamika...how did this crazy bitch find out about Lala? I wondered but then I remembered bumping into her on the basement steps when I was leaving Casper's house the day before. "Man fuck!" I fumed aloud banging my fist on the table. "Ain't this about a bitch!"

"What?" Kisha asked.

I ignored her and replied back to Tamika: **Man what in the fuck do you want from me? I mean what are you trying to accomplish by this bullshit right here? Are you really that fucking thirsty for some dick?**

Tamika: Lol nigga I'm not thirsty but I'm not use to rejection or a nigga playing me like I'm not good enough for him. Meet me later on at the Comfort Inn so that we can talk…See ya later sexy.

Me: What? I ain't meeting you no damn where!

Tamika: Oh you will or I will tell Kisha all about the little pregnant hoe that you have on the side! Trust me you don't want that because from what she has told me your ass already have several strikes and she is only seconds away from taking her kids and telling you to kiss her ass!

I sat there torn between whether I should meet this bitch or just go ahead and come clean with Kisha. I'd never imagined that shit would turn out like this! What in the fuck was I going to do? I looked over at Kisha who was staring at me. I assume she was trying to figure out what was wrong. I knew that I couldn't come clean with her! That shit was totally out of the question! Just as I was about to respond to Tamika another message came through.

Lala: I'm in labor. Call me asap!!!

I looked at my phone unable to believe my luck! This was some straight bullshit!!!

****

THANK YOU'S

First and foremost I would like to thank God for everything. Without him nothing would be possible. I thank him for blessing me with this wonderful gift to be able to write and entertain people with my stories. Secondly, I would like to thank my three beautiful babies, Ny'Ajah, Camari, and AnTeyvion. You three are the reason that I grind so hard and continue to strive for more and to become a better me. I would like to thank my mom, Angela Taylor and my dad, Paul Hill. I am thankful for and appreciate you both. To my grandmothers Ann West and Mable Hill, I love you both and thank you for being there for me whenever I have needed you both. To my sister and my best friend Tinika Taylor, I love you more than life itself. You are my rock, the one person I can depend on when everyone else in this harsh world has turned their backs on me! I treasure every moment that the two of us get to spend together when you are home and when you are away I miss you so badly! Can't wait until you come home! (We have videos to make so that we can entertain the world with our beautiful voices). To all of my aunts, uncles and cousins, I love you guys. R.I.P to my uncles Steve and Calvin, I miss you both very much. A special shout out to my uncle Al Kelly, even though we don't get to see each other much anymore because of our hectic schedules, I love you to pieces and thank you so much for the love and support that you have shown me. Thank you to my sister from another mother Denise Mason, I love you girl and appreciate you. Thanks for listening to my constant drama lol even though I already know what you be saying in your head when I be yapping…lmao! To my cousin, Teresa Porter (my late night, early morning riding partner). Thanks for being there for me the times when I have needed you the most to just be a listening ear.

Now I'd like to thank all of the fans who have followed my work! Thank you to each and every one of you who has ever purchased any of my work or just taken time to read an excerpt of mine. I appreciate it. Thank you to Cash who has believed in a

sista since day one. I can't begin to express to you how much your

friendship and constant advice and support means to me, I love

you. To all of the wonderful authors who have supported me or

just given me advice, thank you. Aaron Bebo, Jason Hooper, Aleta

Williams, Authoress Red, Andrionna Williams, Candice

Stevenson. There are a few of you who have been some real riders

so I definitely have to shout you out. Kendra Littleton, Brandi

McClinton, Novie Cuteyez, Sharon Blount, Skeet the Poet, Karen

Patterson, Chyna Blue, Raychelle Williams, Shayna Williams,

Judy Richburg, and Shaniqua Townes. Shout to one of the best

book clubs BRAB! You guys rock!!! Thank you all so much. If I

have forgotten any one I truly apologize. I suck at this lol. Please

know that it wasn't intentional.

PR

47144864R00147

Made in the USA
Charleston, SC
05 October 2015